Ali –
Happy Not Christmas!

EMERALD HEARTS

ELIANA WEST

Eliana West

FOUR HOLLY DATES

AN EMERALD HEARTS NOVELLA

CHAPTER 1

"Holly Williams, is that you?"

Holly stopped in her tracks. It couldn't be. She hadn't heard that voice since high school. She did a slow turn, and sure enough, Nicholas Anderson walked toward her with that same cocky smile she had spent too many hours daydreaming about as a teenager.

Hugging the tablet, she carried closer to her chest as if it would somehow shield her from his magnetism she blinked up at him. "Hi, Nick."

"Hey, Holly Berry, what in the world are you doing here?"

She grimaced at her old nickname and looked down at her scrubs with pandas printed on the top.

"Nothing much. Just sitting around eating bon-bons and watching *Oprah*," she quipped.

Nick's forehead wrinkled before he burst out laughing. "I guess that was an obvious question. Are you a doctor or a nurse here?"

"I'm a nurse, and as a matter of fact, I've got to get going. Good to see you, Nick."

She waved and did her best to look as though she was walking away quickly instead of running.

As soon as she made it around the corner, she ducked into a supply closet and grabbed onto the metal shelving to steady herself. Nicholas Anderson was in Seattle. How was it the one guy who somehow made her feel even smaller than the rest of the world did, without even trying, was *here*?

Moving all the way across the country from Florida to the Pacific Northwest meant she would never run into anyone from her old life. Or at least that's what she hoped. But here he was, the most popular boy in high school, at her hospital looking even more handsome than he had at graduation. And of course, he still had that smile that made his eyes crinkle in a sexy way. Eyes that were the most amazing shade of blue-gray that always made it hard to focus on what he was saying when he looked directly at her. And why were his shoulders so broad and when did he get so tall?

"Get a hold of yourself," she muttered.

This wasn't high school. Children's Hospital was a big place, and the odds were she wouldn't run into him again. Feeling calmer, Holly took a deep breath and opened the door.

She debated going back in when she saw Nick leaning against the wall, his arms crossed and an amused glint in his eye.

"Forget something, Holly Berry?"

Deep breath. "What are you doing here, Nick?"

"I've been traded to the Seattle Emeralds. My teammate Hugh Donavan mentioned that he tries to do weekly visits with the kids here and I thought I'd come along."

"You're living in Seattle?" Much to her horror, the words came out as a high-pitched squeak.

"I am! I wasn't expecting to run into someone from back

home. Do you know anyone else from Lake Mary who's here?"

She shook her head. "No."

His lips curled into a smile. "I guess it's just us, then."

"Yeah, I guess so." She chewed on her lip. "Well, it was nice to see you again. Bye."

"Wait up." Nick started walking with her. "I'm new here, and other than the guys on the team, I don't know anyone but you. Maybe we could hang out and you could show me around."

"Why?" The question slipped out.

Nick stopped and looked down at her with a frown. "Why? Because we're friends."

"No, we're not. You barely knew who I was in high school. You called me 'Holly Berry,' but I don't know if you know my actual name. We definitely weren't friends."

She felt a small tinge of guilt for her outburst when Nick's face fell.

"That's not how I remember it," he said quietly.

She sighed. "Nick, we never hung out together."

"But you came to all the soccer games. I always saw you up at the top of the stands." He frowned. "Until junior year and then I barely saw you."

"I started taking classes at the community college. Which you would have known if we had been friends."

"You could do that?"

"There's a program called Running Start. It let me take college classes along with my high school classes. I was able to graduate high school with my associate's degree."

"Wow, you were in a hurry."

"You kind of have to be when you're a foster kid. I had to take advantage of the free education while I could."

And there was that look of pity. Which was why she didn't share that piece of information with many people.

"I didn't know."

Holly shrugged. "Like I said, we weren't friends. Why would you?"

Before he could answer, her name—her real name—rang out over the intercom.

"I've gotta go. Good luck with the team," she called over her shoulder as she headed down the hallway.

She spent the rest of her day replaying her conversation with Nick. As the shock of seeing him wore off, she wondered if he would come to the hospital as often as his teammate Hugh Donavan and if he did, how she could avoid making a fool of herself again?

A frustrated groan escaped. She'd been making aimless circles around her apartment since she got home from her shift, trying to process the jumble of emotions seeing Nick again brought on. She had been short with him, which wasn't like her. Seeing the flash of hurt in his eyes when she said they weren't friends caught her by surprise. She'd always assumed Nick wasn't aware of her in school. Discovering that he remembered her brought on a warm feeling of satisfaction that was unfamiliar and unsettling.

She glanced toward the kitchen. The last thing she wanted to do was make herself dinner. Plus, cooking for one wasn't very fun. Pulling out her phone, she hesitated for just a minute before she decided it was worth the splurge and called the restaurant. With dinner on the way, she sent a text to her neighbor. Poornima knocked on her door a minute later.

"Tell me again about when you opened the door and he was waiting for you in the hallway," Poornima said, popping another dumpling into her mouth.

Holly groaned and pushed away her half-eaten container

of fried rice away. "I have never been so embarrassed in my entire life."

"Remind me to tell you about the first time I tried to cook for Rajeev and forgot to put the fish in the fish curry. I mean, who does that?"

Holly laughed. "That is a good one."

"Nick Anderson was the golden boy in high school, right?"

"He was one of those popular kids who had everything—nice family, money, and good looking."

"And now he's looking at you." Poornima waggled her eyebrows.

"I don't know why. I didn't think he even knew who I was in high school."

"Why not? I picture you being just as beautiful then as you are now."

Holly smiled a little. She hadn't changed much since school. Her hair fell around her shoulders in the same mix of curls and waves, and she could still fit into her favorite pair of jeans she wore back then. People still asked her, "What are you?" as they tried to make sense of her light brown skin and amber colored eyes. Her mother's Puerto Rican roots and her father being Black gave her a look that simply didn't fit into any specific box.

"Thanks, that's nice of you to say. And thank you for coming over to have dinner with me."

"I'm glad you asked. Rajeev is working tonight and it's not asking too much for me to walk across the driveway."

Holly rented a small apartment above Poornima and Rajeev Sankar's garage. It had been a stroke of luck when Dr. Sankar overheard her talking about looking for a place to live with one of the other nurses when she first started working at the hospital. Over the years, Rajeev and his wife Poornima had become good friends, and she considered them as close as any family she'd ever had.

She sighed. "Hopefully, it was just a one-time thing and I won't run into him again."

"I don't think you're going to get your wish."

"What makes you say that?"

"The guy waited for you outside of a supply closet. My auntie would tell you that's definitely a sign that he's interested."

Holly rolled her eyes. "I'm sure you're wrong on this one."

"You may not be Indian, but I am going to be your honorary auntie, and I'm telling you I'm right."

Holly shook her head but then looked at Poornima with wide eyes after she cracked open her fortune cookie.

"What does it say?"

Holly handed her friend the fortune and then took a huge sip of wine while Poornima read it out loud.

"You will run into an old friend again."

CHAPTER 2

Holly Williams was in Seattle. Nick put the address of the pub where he was meeting Hugh in his GPS and headed to a neighborhood close to the hospital. He was so preoccupied by running into Holly again he walked right past the table where his teammate Hugh Donavan sat.

"Nick," Hugh called out.

Nick backtracked and dropped into the booth. "Sorry, man. I was just a little distracted."

"Here." Hugh pushed a bottle of beer toward him. "I went ahead and ordered for you."

"Thanks, man." He looked around at the wood paneled walls and vintage green vinyl booths. "This place is cool."

"A lot of the doctors and nurses from the hospital hang out here after their shift. It's close to the hospital and they have a great craft beer menu."

Nick took a swig of the dark amber-colored liquid and nodded in appreciation. Seattle's breweries were some of the best in the country, a bonus to being traded to the Emeralds.

"What's got you so distracted?" Hugh asked. "It's okay if

meeting with the kids was too much for you. Not everyone can handle being around seriously ill children."

"No, it's not that," Nick answered. "The kids were great and I'm happy I got the chance to visit with them." He took a large swig of his beer and took a deep breath. "I ran into a classmate from high school when we were at the hospital."

"That must have been a pleasant surprise."

"I guess it wasn't as nice for her as it was for me."

Hugh looked at him expectantly.

"Holly Williams." He shook his head regretfully. "I thought we were friends, but I guess I was wrong."

"I know Holly—she works with my girlfriend Noelle. They go kayaking together sometimes."

Maybe that could be the break Nick needed.

Hugh cocked his head. "You weren't one of the kids who called her 'Holly Berry,' were you? She mentioned that to Noelle."

So much for that break. Nick rubbed the back of his neck. "Well, we all kind of called her that."

Hugh frowned. "She hated that, you know."

"I know now and it's not going to help my chances getting her to go out with me."

The beer churned in Nick's stomach. All this time he assumed everyone had had as much fun in high school as he did.

"You're not off to a very good start, are you?" Hugh laughed. "Let me give you some advice. This isn't a sprint. It took me months to get Noelle to go out on a date with me. And I'm not exaggerating. *Months.*"

Nick nodded and sighed. "So you're saying I need to be patient."

"If you're interested in her and it sounds to me like you

are, then yes. Persistence and patience are going to be your best bet."

"Got it."

"I'm assuming that means you'll be coming back to the hospital with me next week?"

Nick raised his glass. "Absolutely."

He appreciated Hugh taking him under his wing. He knew some of the other guys on the team but wasn't close with any of them. Hugh had picked him up at the airport when he flew out for his first visit and they clicked right away. Good thing, since they both played midfield.

They parted ways after a couple of rounds. Nick felt a small pang of jealousy at Hugh's eagerness to get back to the hospital to pick Noelle up after her shift. He wanted to be that excited to see someone at the end of the day.

That evening, the white peaks of the Olympic Mountains glowed pale pink in the light of the setting sun. The mountains merged with sky and water in a way that had taken Nick's breath away the first time he had seen the view, and every time since then.

He stood in front of the floor-to-ceiling window of the executive hotel room he was staying in while he looked for his own place. Seeing this view, he could understand how people came to Seattle for a visit and ended up staying. He'd only been in the city a month and he'd already fallen under its spell. And that was in the winter. Hugh had told him that a summers in the Pacific Northwest were magical.

Sitting down in a chair facing the window, Nick opened his laptop. He quickly discovered Holly had only one social media account. He smiled as he scrolled through her pictures on Instagram. Most of her posts involved hiking, cross-country skiing, and kayaking, but there was one picture he kept coming back to over and over again.

It was a selfie she'd taken out on the water, on what must have been a summer day. The wind tousled her soft curls and her skin glowed golden brown. Bare arms under her life vest revealed well toned limbs from the exercise. Her full lips were pulled into a smile and she squinted against the sun's glare on the water.

Looking at the picture, made him eager for summer and the chance to share a sunny day on the water with Holly.

It was the eyes he remembered the most from high school, beautiful amber eyes. Holly had had this way of looking at him that always made him feel as though she saw him as something more than the popular athlete. She never tried to flirt with him the way almost every other girl in school did, never went out of her way to get his attention. She always walked down the hall with her books clasped to her chest. But every once in a while, her eyes would flick up and connect with his. And he remembered those eyes.

With a few more clicks he found their yearbooks online. He looked through all four years, but only found one candid picture of her. There she was just the way he remembered her, at the top corner of the stands. While the rest of his classmates were shouting and cheering during a football game against their archrival, she had had her head bent over a book.

He pulled out his phone. He knew one person who might be able to answer some of the many questions he had about Holly Williams.

"Hey, Mom."

"Nick! Hi, sweetie. It's late—is everything okay?"

He winced and glanced at the top of his phone. "Sorry, I didn't even think about the time. I'm still getting used to the time difference."

"That's okay, I'm just finishing up making cookies for the bake sale."

Nick smiled. This was why he called his mother. Rebecca Anderson was the embodiment of the school mom who volunteered for everything and had served in every PTA board position, including president. With one child left in the school system, she was still going strong.

"I have a question for you. I ran into Holly Williams today. Do you remember her?"

"Of course I do. She was an amazing young woman."

"I didn't know she was a foster kid."

There was a moment of silence. "Nick, your father and I could give you, your brother, and sisters a nice childhood with many advantages. The disadvantage of that is that you assumed everyone else had the same kind of life."

"Do you know what happened? Why she ended up in foster care?"

"I do, but I don't think it would be appropriate for me to share. If you want to know, you should ask her. What I *can* tell you is that I remember her so well because she was one of the hardest-working kids I ever met. She took college courses along with her regular high school classes and she graduated with a full scholarship to study nursing."

"Well, she accomplished her goal, because she's a nurse. Remember, I told you I was going to visit kids at Children's Hospital with my teammate Hugh? She works there."

"Oh, I am so happy to hear that," his mom exclaimed. "I bet she's still just as pretty as she was in high school."

"She's beautiful."

"Please tell me you didn't use that silly nickname you kids had for her. What was it you called her, Holly Berry?"

When he didn't answer, his mother groaned. "Oh, Nick."

CHAPTER 3

Holly closed her eyes and lifted her face to the light. It was one of those rare November days where the sun was shining, the sky was bright blue, and the temperatures were unseasonably warm. She took advantage and brought her lunch outside into one of the gardens on the hospital grounds.

Something moved next to her, but she ignored it. She squeezed her eyes closed tighter when she heard Nick's voice.

"Hi, Holly."

She sighed. "Hi, Nick."

"I haven't seen you in a couple of weeks."

Reluctantly, she pried her eyes open and looked straight into those blue-gray eyes that always made her whole body fizzle and pop like a shaken bottle of soda.

"I guess we haven't been on the same schedule," she answered.

He didn't need to know that Holly had switched shifts to make sure it was that way.

Nick was sitting on the bench across from her, his forearms on his knees and his hands clasped in front of him. He was wearing sweats and a Seattle Emeralds sweatshirt. The colors complimented his light brown hair and made his eyes stand out even more.

"Any plans for Thanksgiving?" he asked.

"I'll be working."

He rubbed his hands together. "Oh, well, there's a team Christmas party in a couple of weeks."

"I'm not really into Christmas and all of that stuff."

"If you don't like parties, I hear they do a big tree lighting ceremony downtown—maybe we could—"

"I don't celebrate Christmas."

Nick wrinkled his forehead. "Are you Jewish?"

Holly bit back a smile. "No, I just don't like Christmas."

"Well, maybe that's because—"

She groaned and held up her hand. "Please don't turn into that guy."

"What guy?"

"That guy who thinks he's going to show the girl the magic of Christmas. You know, the one in all the holiday movies they start showing in July. I'm just one of those people who doesn't like all the fuss. Pine needles are messy and then it's all this hype for one day, and…" She shrugged. "Sorry, I just don't get it."

Nick stared at her for a minute and then dipped his chin. "Okay, so no Christmas."

"You're not going to try to convince me I'm missing out?"

"Nope."

"That's new," she muttered.

"We can still hang out," he went on, undaunted. "If you don't want to do Christmas stuff, what would you rather do?"

He leaned closer and his shoulder bumped against hers. “What do you like to do?”

What do you like to do?

Holly blinked, her gaze locked on the corner of his lip that curled up just slightly. She took a breath, trying to keep from letting the clean citrus and woodsy scent from his cologne or body wash or whatever it was that made him smell so damn good distract her even more than it already did.

When the lip curled into a smile, she realized she’d been staring.

“I…”

“What would you rather do than celebrate Christmas?” he asked again.

“Go cross-country skiing, kayaking, stargazing, all sorts of things.” She shrugged.

He nodded as she ran down her list. “Okay, got it.”

This was ridiculous. What did it matter to him what she’d rather do than celebrate Christmas?

“There are four weeks in December. I figure we can hang out every weekend…” He frowned. “Unless you have other plans. Or are you working? Wait a minute. I didn’t think this through. How about this—four weeks in December, we get to hang out at least once each week.”

He grinned at her and nodded as if everything he just said made perfect sense.

She stared at him. “What?” Holly drew back.

“Don’t worry, we’re not going to do Christmas stuff.”

She shook her head. “That’s not the problem. I don’t understand why you want to hang out with me.”

“You’re the only person I know in Seattle besides the team, I think you’re funny, I think you’re beautiful, I want to get to know you better, I like you, all sorts of reasons.”

She stared at him while he mimicked her list, except each

thing on his list took her by surprise. Nick thought she was all of those things?

Her heart began to hammer and her mouth went dry. She couldn't have said anything in response, even if she wanted to.

"Well, what do you think?"

"I...okay."

"Great." Nick held his hand out. "Give me your phone and I'll put in my number."

On auto pilot, she handed over her phone. Nick gave it back to her a minute later and jumped up.

"Sorry I've gotta run, I'm late, I'll see you later!"

And with that, Nick jogged across to the parking lot and climbed into a sleek black sports car, waving as he drove by.

She stared at her phone where Nick had stored his number.

What the hell had just happened?

"Holly, are you okay?" Her friend and co-worker Thanh asked when she got back to the nurses' station, still confused.

"I...don't know."

Her friend and co-worker Noelle, came over and put her hand on her shoulder. "What's going on?"

"I just agreed to go on four dates with Nick Anderson."

Noelle and Thanh exchanged a look and they both smiled.

"That's a good thing, right?" Thanh asked.

"I've never been on a date," Holly revealed.

This time the two friends exchanged worried looks.

"You've never been on a date, like *ever*?" Thanh asked.

"I was too busy in high school, add to that having it drilled into me by every foster parent and social worker I ever had that I didn't want to end up a statistic, so I just..." Holly shrugged.

Noelle put her arm around her. "Do you *want* to go on a date with Nick?"

"Maybe…I don't know. I'm just… Nick was the golden boy in high school. Every girl crushed on him. I just…" Holly sighed. "This feels very Cinderella-ish, and I've never believed in fairy tales."

"It seems too good to be true," Noelle said with an understanding nod. "I felt the same way when I agreed to go out on a date with Hugh, but I'm so glad I did."

Thanh cleared his throat. "Only because your best friend gave you a little push."

Noelle grinned and rolled her eyes. "Yes, of course. Thank you, Thanh."

"So you both think I should go?" Holly asked. She started feeling a little anxious, now that the shock was abating.

"I think that you should listen to your heart," Noelle said.

"And your friends," Thanh added. "Maybe it's time to start believing in fairy tales."

"Don't you dare start calling me 'Cinderella.' " She wagged her finger at Thanh.

"Okay." He walked away but called over his shoulder, "Bye, Cindi," in a singsong voice.

CHAPTER 4

"Are you getting settled in okay?" Hugh asked.

"Yeah, I am. It's a lot colder than I'm used to, but I think I'm getting the hang of dressing in layers."

Hugh laughed. "That's practically an art form in the Pacific Northwest." He passed the ball back to Nick. "Any luck finding a place?"

"There are a couple of good prospects. Thanks for hooking me up with the real estate agent, by the way."

They ran down the indoor practice field for the Emeralds, passing the ball back and forth.

"Did you know Holly had a big crush on you in high school?" Hugh panted.

Nick froze. Hugh made a hard pass that he would have returned if he hadn't been trying to process what his teammate just told him. The ball hit him right in the stomach instead making him double over.

"What?" he wheezed, trying to catch his breath.

Hugh jogged over and bent to look at him. "You okay?"

"Yeah, I — I just got distracted there for a minute."

Hugh grimaced. "I shouldn't have told you that. Don't tell Holly I said anything, okay?"

Nick waved his hand, still trying to take a full breath. "Got it."

Hugh dropped to the turf and started doing stretches. "So, did you know?"

Nick sat opposite Hugh and mirrored his movements. "No, apparently there's a lot I don't know about Holly, but I'm trying to learn."

"And you still managed to get her to agree to four dates. Nice move, man."

Nick leaned back on his palms and grinned, taking a deep breath. "Thanks. Now I just have to figure out what we're going to do."

Hugh snorted and shook his head. "Two women named Noelle and Holly who don't like Christmas. Go figure."

Nick raised his eyebrows. "Noelle too?"

"Yup." Hugh laughed and stretched.

"So what do you have planned for you and Noelle this holiday season?" Nick needed ideas, and fast.

"I'm taking her sailing up in the San Juans."

"Nice. I just have to come up with four dates that have nothing to do with the holidays."

Hugh cocked his head. "Do you?"

Nick stopped and stared at him. "What do you mean?"

"There's something like twenty other holidays in December, dude. What if you did something for some of those?"

Nick brightened, nodding. "I like where you're going with this."

"Come on." Hugh stood up and put out a hand down to him. "Let's grab a couple of smoothies and do some research."

It turned out there were a *lot* of holidays in December.

Some were religious, some were serious, and some were just silly. Heartened, Nick thanked Hugh and left the training facility with a list. Now all he had to do was plan the dates.

His phone buzzed on his way out of the training facility and he grinned when he saw the name on the caller ID.

"Hey, big brother, how's it going?"

"Good, we're in," his brother Jason paused and mumbled to himself. "Denver. I've got one more show to do here and then we head to… Oh hell, this tour has been so grueling I don't know which way is up anymore," he said with a tired laugh. "I've got some time, the opening act just went on, so I thought I'd try to catch up."

"You sure you're holding up okay?"

"You know how it is when you're on the road. Sometimes it gets hard to remember where you are. I'll be able to catch up on some sleep when I come home for the holiday break."

"You've been on the road for almost a year now. Maybe you need a longer break than just the holidays."

His brother sighed. "You're right."

"Isn't the last show in Vancouver? Maybe you can come down and visit when you're done."

"I'll think about it. Hey, Mom called and said you ran into Holly Williams."

"I did."

"Mom said she thought you wanted to ask her out."

Nick groaned. If his mom said something to his brother, then the entire family knew.

"Brace yourself," Jason said with a laugh. "You're going to get the third degree at Thanksgiving, you know that."

As much as he looked forward to spending the holiday with his family, Nick couldn't help wondering what Holly would be doing. He chatted with his brother for a few more minutes until he heard the roar of the crowd in the background and Jason announced that he had to go.

Nick stared at the phone for a minute afterward, debating with himself before he scrolled through his contacts and sent a quick text. He waited, watching the three bubbles at the bottom of the screen. When he saw the answer, he couldn't help smiling.

"Why did you want to meet me for coffee?" Holly asked again, repeating her answer to his text.

They were sitting in one of the hospital coffee shops an hour after he messaged her.

"Does there have to be a reason?"

She picked at the sleeve on her cup. "No, I guess not."

"So, how long have you worked here?"

"Three years now. One of my professors in nursing school helped me get a job here."

"Why didn't you stay back home and get a job there?"

"There wasn't anything to keep me in Lake Mary. I wanted to start over in a place where I wouldn't hear people whisper about that 'poor Williams girl.' "

"I'm sorry."

There was sadness in her eyes, but also determination when she looked at him. "Don't be. I'm lucky—I had some wonderful people who mentored me. I was able to get a full scholarship and I took advantage of any program I could find. When you're a foster kid, you age out of the system when you turn eighteen. By the time I graduated I had found enough resources to end up better off than a lot of kids in my situation."

"So no family at all?"

"None that I want to have anything to do with."

The words *I'm sorry* sat on the tip of his tongue. Nick bit his cheek to keep them there. He nodded and sipped at his coffee while he got his emotions in check.

"About these dates…" Holly started tentatively. "Am I going to have to dress up? I can if I need to, but I don't really have any dresses. I could get one, but if I don't have to I'd rather not. I…" Her cheeks reddened. "I'll stop talking now."

Nick reached across the table and put his hand over hers, where it rested on top of a small pile of shredded cardboard that once was the sleeve surrounding her coffee cup. "I spend most of my life in sweats. I only wear a suit when I have to or when my mother makes me. We'll keep it casual, okay?"

'Thanks."

"I almost forgot. I'm supposed to say hi from my mom."

Holly smiled. "I always liked your mom. She wrote a really nice letter of recommendation for me for my scholarship application."

"She did? She didn't mention that."

"Your mom was one of my mentors through high school and set me up with another mentor when I went to college."

Nick sat back. "I had no idea."

"That was one of the things I liked about your mom. I would talk to her the most because I knew she wasn't going to say anything. I hated it when people would talk about me behind my back."

"I feel bad that I didn't know."

"You shouldn't. I wouldn't have wanted you to."

"Thank you for sharing with me now."

Her eyes dropped to where he still had his hand on hers and she quickly pulled it away. She looked at her watch.

"I have to get back to work."

He threw their cups in the garbage and walked out of the coffee shop with her.

"I'll pick you up Thursday morning. It's going to be cold, so wear something warm and shoes you can walk or hike in."

"Can I get any other hint about where we're going?"

"Nope. You're just going to have to trust me."

Holly cocked her head and studied him for a minute. "I think I can do that."

CHAPTER 5

"I thought it would be a good idea if we started with something simple," Nick said, pulling up to a small building on Lake Union.

He jumped out of the car and ran around to open the door for her. Holly got out before he got there and looked around, trying to figure out where they were going. He grasped her hand.

"Wait, what are we doing?" She stopped when he started toward the building with the Kenmore Air logo on the side.

"We're doing an air tour of Puget Sound."

Holly's jaw dropped. "We can't do that."

"Why not?"

"Because it's too extravagant."

"Fine, I'll say I got a Groupon if that will make you feel better. Besides, I'm new in town and this is a great way for me to get the lay of the land. Right?"

Holly shook her head. "I…"

Nick tugged on her hand. "Come on, we're going to be late."

Before she could think of another reason to say no, he

whisked inside where an attendant greeted them before leading them out to the dock.

"Ladies first," Nick said.

Holly climbed into the small plane and put on the headset the pilot provided for her. She looked around, her stomach feeling a little jumpy. The few times she had flown was on a commercial plane; she'd never been in a plane this small before.

Nick got in and they sat shoulder to shoulder in the small compartment. Their gazes met, his eyes sparkling with excitement as he put his own headset on. Once the pilot gave them the safety instructions, he started the motor and the plane bobbed along the waves of the lake, picking up speed as it gradually lifted into the air.

No, this was no giant jet at *all.*

Holly gasped and grabbed Nick's hand when her stomach dipped as the ground dropped away.

His voice crackled through the headset. "Are you okay?"

Taking a deep breath, she nodded and looked out of the window at the blue-gray waters of the lakes below. It was one of those rare winter days when the skies were crystal clear and the sun made a surprise appearance.

Nick tapped her shoulder and when she turned around, he was looking at her with a serious expression. "I have something to tell you. We are celebrating a holiday today."

What was he doing? Holly tried to pull her hand away, but he trapped it between his.

"Happy International Civil Aviation Day," he announced.

She stared at him for a minute while her brain processed what he just said. Then a bubble of laughter burst out. She shook her head, unable to contain her grin.

"It's not dancing, skiing, kayaking, or stargazing, but I figured this could count in the 'all sorts of things' category."

"This definitely counts as all sorts of things," she agreed.

They spent the next forty-five minutes flying over the San Juan Islands, with the pilot pointing out different landmarks along the way, some of which Holly was unfamiliar with. When the pilot instructed them to prepare for landing, she gave Nick a questioning look.

"Lunch," he announced.

The plane descended onto the water and the pilot announced that they arrived at Orcas Island. The largest of the group of islands known as the San Juans, it wasn't as densely populated as many others. Holly thought about taking the ferry to visit one day but it didn't seem like it would be fun to visit alone. She glanced at Nick. He was the last person she imagined taking this trip with, but as the plane taxied to the dock, she was happy to share this experience with him.

Nick got out, reaching for her arm as she followed suit, her legs wobbling on the dock. The motion of the plane combined with the gentle sway of the dock had her clutching her middle.

"Come on, let's stretch our legs a bit. It's less than a mile into town and it will give our stomachs a chance to settle before we eat."

"I've wanted to come here ever since I moved to Seattle," Holly said, taking in the natural beauty that surrounded them. Dense evergreen forest covered most of the land, with just a few small towns dotting the island. It was even more enchanting in person than what she had seen in pictures.

She tugged her hat down over her ears when the breeze picked up. "Now I know why you told me to wear something warm."

Nick wrapped his arm around her shoulders. "I was really worried it was going to rain. I was watching the forecast for the last week with my fingers crossed. We'll definitely have to come back here in the summer when it's warmer."

Holly's heart jumped at that. He was so excited about this. Nick was enthusiastic about everything—he always had been. It was one of the things she had always liked about him.

She had never been that carefree, mainly because she couldn't afford to be. Caution had been her watchword most of her life.

It didn't take long for them to reach town. They wandered in and out of a couple of shops, Nick's enthusiasm for all the local crafts was infectious. At each stop he offered to buy her something but she declined. There was nothing he could give her that meant more to her than having this time together. He bought a beautiful bowl for his mom at a pottery shop and a book for his dad on the history of the islands at the local bookstore before they settled in at a restaurant with a view of the water. They took full advantage of the local seafood and shared an enormous bowl of clams seasoned with butter and garlic.

Lunch had never tasted so good. She knew it wasn't the food, the wine, or the setting. It had everything to do with the person sitting on the other side of the table.

Nick laced her fingers with his on the way back to the dock. Their seaplane hadn't arrived to take them back yet, so they walked along the shore for a little way looking at sea shells. She watched in amazement when Nick pointed at a seal that had poked its head out of the water, watching them with large black eyes. It was getting dark—the days were markedly shorter this late in the year—and when Holly saw the lights of the plane in the distance, she was torn, suddenly not wanting the trip to end yet.

Nick stood in front of her and ran his hands up and down her arms.

"I wish we had more time. Thank you for coming here with me today."

He leaned toward her and she knew he was going to kiss her.

Holly took a deep breath. This was going to be awkward. But could it be more embarrassing than if Nick kissed her and having him think she was a really terrible kisser instead of just completely clueless?

She exhaled and leaned back. "The thing is… The thing is this is my first date ever, so when I say I don't kiss on the first date, it's not because I'm being old-fashioned, it's because…I've never kissed anybody."

Holly didn't know what she said next, so she just kept nervously talking until Nick gently grasped her by the shoulders. "Holly, stop. You're not going to scare me away, no matter how hard you try. I'm sorry that you missed out on all the firsts you should have had back in school. Your first dance, your first date…your first kiss. But I'm selfish." He laughed softly. "My mom would tell you I always have been. Now I get to be the one who gives you some of those firsts…" He moved his hands down her arms and took her hands in his. "If you'll let me."

She blinked back the tears that threatened to fall. "I…" She let her forehead fall to his chest and exhaled.

Nick wrapped his arms around her and pulled her close. "It's okay, sweetheart," he murmured.

Her voice was muffled in Nick's chest. "A guy never said that to me, either."

"Another first for me." He stepped back and lifted her chin until his eyes met his.

"I don't want to do anything to ruin this day," he said. "And you're right, you shouldn't kiss on the first date." He smiled. "Not even me."

Nick glanced over her shoulder. "The plane's here. It's time to head home."

On the way home, the confines of the plane felt much smaller. The dimensions hadn't changed, but her awareness of Nick had. Each time he shifted and his leg or shoulder brushed against hers, Holly felt a tingling that spread through her body.

She was frustrated with herself for not letting him kiss her. Her cautious nature once again getting in the way of her enjoying her life.

"Wow, what an amazing view," he said, squeezing her hand as the city lights came into view.

Seattle on a clear winter evening was an incredible sight. The Space Needle glowed in shades of blue and white, welcoming them back as the plane descended onto Lake Union.

They thanked the pilot and Nick escorted her back to his car.

"Everything all right?" he asked after Holly sighed for the second time on their way back to her apartment.

"I'm just sorry to have the day end," she said with a smile. "Thank you for asking me out."

"We have three more dates. This is just the beginning."

He pulled up to her apartment and jumped out to open the door for her and walk her to the stairs.

He reached up and brushed the hair out of her eyes. "I had a great time today. Happy International Civil Aviation Day."

Nick reached into his pocket and handed her a small package wrapped in paper with little airplanes on it.

Holly turned the box over in her hand. "What is this?"

"Just a little something for you to remember our day."

Still mystified, she carefully peeled the paper away from the box and folded it, tucking it into her pocket. Then she lifted the lid off the box and gasped when she saw the gold necklace with the tiny airplane charm.

She looked up at him, eyes wide. “It’s beautiful, Nick, but you shouldn’t have.”

“Like I said, I wanted you to have something to remember today.”

She’d never been given a piece of jewelry before.

He leaned toward her, his warm breath fanning her cheek. “Good night, Holly.”

Nick pressed his lips to her cheek before he returned to his car and drove away.

Holly looked from the necklace to where Nick’s taillights had just disappeared and back to the jewelry again. She was in serious danger of being swept off her feet, and it was only the first date. What in the world was Nick going to come up with for the next one?

CHAPTER 6

Nick rubbed his hands together and paced in front of his car, waiting for Holly to come down the stairs from her apartment.

Holly's landlord walked over. Nick had met Dr. Sankar during his trips to the hospital, and they had spoken from time to time, since it turned out that Rajeev was a soccer fan. "Hey, Nick! So is this date number two?"

Nick shook Dr. Sankar's hand. "Yep."

"Our whole unit has been wondering what you've got planned after International Civil Aviation Day. Nice move, by the way."

Nick grinned. "Thanks."

Rajeev rubbed his hands together. "Any hints?"

"Nope."

"Holly's a great girl and we all care about her." Rajeev's tone grew serious. "She's worked really hard and doesn't take the time to have as much fun as she should. So, I'm happy to see her going out, but—"

Nick held his hands up. "I promise I'll be a gentleman, you don't have to worry."

Rajeev gave him a wry smile. "I'm not the one you have to be concerned about. My wife Poornima will unleash all of her aunties on you if you hurt our girl."

"Thanks for the warning."

With that, Rajeev tipped his chin to where Holly was coming down the stairs.

Nick's heart stuttered as he watched her coming toward him. Today, she was wearing skinny jeans and brown boots with a chunky gray sweater. She had her hair piled on top of her head, with a few tendrils framing her face and brushing against the floral scarf that she had wound around her neck. Her coat over one arm, she approached him with a bright smile.

"Don't let Rajeev try to get any information out of you about our date. I know the whole unit was placing bets on what you've got planned for today."

"Hey, I've got five dollars riding on this," Rajeev exclaimed.

Nick laughed. "Maybe next time."

Rajeev gave him a conspiratorial smile. "Maybe."

Nick held out his hand for Holly. "Ready?"

He bit back a smile when she slipped her hand into his without hesitation. They had exchanged a few text messages, but he'd tried not to seem too eager. If it had been up to him, he'd find any excuse to talk to her, morning, noon, and night.

She was bluntly honest and it was a refreshing change from other women he had dated. Nick discovered that because of her childhood she was hyper aware of how much things cost and uncomfortable with extravagance. She mentioned the cost of their trip to Orcas Island for their first date more than once, so for date number two, he decided to dial it back a bit.

Sure enough, as they were pulling out of the driveway,

she asked, "We're not going to do anything too expensive this time, are we?"

"No airplanes this time, I promise."

This time he drove to another part of the city and pulled up to a low building on a side street in Ballard.

She looked at the sign and then looked at him with a raised eyebrow. "Chocolate?"

"Happy Chocolate Covered Anything Day."

Like last time, he pulled out another little box, this one wrapped in paper with assorted chocolates on it, and handed it to her.

She shook her head but her lips quirked, and even though she tried to fight it, she started to laugh. "Thank you, Nick," she finally said.

Just like the first time, she took care to unwrap the box. This time, lifting the lid revealed a small silver strawberry charm dipped in gold instead of chocolate.

"Thank you, Nick," she said again as she took her necklace off and added the charm to it, nestling it next to the tiny airplane he had given her last time. A glance at the side mirror allowed her to see the necklace, now with two charms glinting.

He got out and came around to open her door and offer her his hand.

"You don't have to do that, you know," she said.

"Do what?"

"Open the door for me."

He pulled back to let her get out. "Are you kidding me? My mother would have my hide if I didn't act like a gentleman. She's serious about it. One time when she was at one of my brother's shows, she actually got up and went backstage and barged into the dressing room and cussed my brother out when she saw him push one of the backup singers out of his way to get off the stage."

"Oh, no."

"Yup. It was when he first started getting big. She said she didn't raise a self-indulgent rock star and if he thought she wouldn't get up on the stage and call him out during the show next time, he was wrong. When Mom goes to one of Jason's shows, his manager always tells security to stay out of her way if she looks mad."

"That's the kind of mom I want to be someday."

Nick paused. "Do you want to have kids?"

"I think so, someday. With the right person."

He'd never pictured himself having kids, not until now. The image of the two of them kicking a soccer ball around the back yard with a little boy and girl felt so right it felt like a punch to the gut.

Their eyes met. Her cheeks flushed that adorable shade of pink that he loved to see on her.

The door opened and a woman in an apron poked her head out. "Are you Mr. Anderson? We're ready for you."

The spell was broken. He put his arm around Holly's shoulder and led her into the chocolate factory.

A couple of hours later, they came out buzzing from a sugar high. They had had a private tour of the factory and then a special tasting with one of their chocolatiers. The company had set out an assortment of things for them to cover in chocolate, and they had a blast coming up with wacky combinations.

Holly looked down at the boxes of different chocolate in her hands. "I can't believe how much chocolate they gave us."

"We'll never be able to eat all of this."

"Would you mind if I took some to the hospital?" she asked.

"Of course not."

"Maybe we could ship some to your mom and dad?"

He couldn't resist the urge to give her a quick kiss on the forehead. "They would love that."

Once they put the boxes in the trunk, Holly turned to him and asked, "Have you ever been to the Ballard locks?"

Well, that was a new one. "What are the Ballard locks?"

Holly grinned at him. "It's one of my favorite places in Seattle." She looked toward the horizon. "There's not too much daylight left, but it's not far."

"Great! Let's go."

It encouraged him that Holly suggested extending their date. It didn't matter where she wanted to go, as long as they were going together. She gave him directions and in just a few minutes, they arrived at a small park next to the water.

The air was clear and brisk along the water as they walked along the canal, where boats went through a gate that allowed them to be lowered from Lake Union to sea level and the same process was reversed for boats coming in from Puget Sound into the lake system. They watched a large barge slowly enter the locks and rise before making its way through the canal to the lake.

"It's much busier during the summer," Holly said, smiling. "I love to come and watch all the different boats go through. Hugh offered to take me sailing and said we could go through the locks when he and Noelle are out on his boat next summer."

Seeing the excitement in her eyes, Nick made a mental note to look into buying a boat. He wanted to be the one to share the experience with Holly.

As they walked around the locks, the sun set and the water became an inky blue. Holly's face became bathed in moonlight and her breath came out in puffs of air. She stopped and whirled around to face him.

She licked her lips. "Nick, this is our second date and I said I don't kiss on the first date. But this is our second date and… I think I want you to kiss me."

He didn't see any uncertainty in her gaze now, only desire. Slowly he leaned forward and, cupping her cheeks, brushed his lips against his. Despite the cold, they were soft and warm, enticing him to delve deeper, but he pulled back, searching her face for any sign of hesitation.

"I just want to make sure you want to—"

Before he could finish, she grabbed his jacket and stood on her tiptoes, and she returned his gentle kiss with much more intensity. There was no hesitation. She let him know with the tiniest flick of her tongue against the seam of his lips she was ready, and he opened his mouth, eager to let her in.

He pulled her against his chest, and her moan reverberated through him, igniting a blaze within him he wanted to let burn bright against the cold winter night.

When they finally pulled apart, her lips were swollen and wet.

"So that's what that feels like. I don't know why I waited for so long," she whispered.

Nick didn't know he had caveman instincts until they flared to life with Holly's words. He drew her toward him, crushing her to him as he pressed his mouth to hers.

When he ended the kiss, he growled, "Because you were waiting for me."

Her fingers trembled when she brushed her fingers over his mouth. She gave a slight nod.

"I was waiting for you."

He sighed, and pressed his forehead to hers. He had two more dates to show Holly Williams that he'd been waiting for her his entire life.

CHAPTER 7

Holly knew she was smiling like a fool, but she couldn't help it and she didn't really want to stop. She'd never been swept off her feet before and she wanted to enjoy every minute of it.

Just as she came out of her patient's room, she ran into Noelle in the hallway.

Her friend looked her up and down. "I don't know if I've ever seen you look so happy. I take it the second date with Nick went well?"

Holly glanced up and down the corridor to make sure there weren't too many prying ears before she leaned over and whispered, "We kissed."

"And?"

"It was amazing," Holly said, sighing with happiness.

Kissing Nick was more than amazing. Real life was so much better than any fantasy she'd ever had in high school about kissing Nick. Those fantasies had been as innocent as she was back then. They hadn't had the heat and passion she'd experienced when he took her in his arms. Nick was gentle, but he made sure she knew with each touch and caress how much he desired her.

"When is your next date? Earth to Holly," Noelle called out, waving her hand in her face.

"Oh, sorry. I was just…thinking."

"Daydreaming is more like it." Noelle laughed.

Holly put her hands on her cheeks to cover her blush. "Is this how you felt with Hugh?"

Now it was Noelle's turn to blush. "I guarded my heart for a long time and I honestly didn't think I would ever feel like this. Even with my ex-husband, I never…" Her eyes became bright with unshed tears. She shook her head and turned away.

Holly put her arm around her friend's shoulder. "I'm sorry. I didn't mean to bring up bad memories for you."

"These aren't sad tears. I'm happier than I ever thought I could be." Noelle sniffed. "I'll never regret giving Hugh a chance, and I hope you feel the same way about Nick."

"I do. I was so focused on surviving for a long time I forgot how to live. Even having a nice home and a good job, I kept my head down and kept working. Other than going for a hike once in a while and kayaking with you, I haven't done anything just for fun, just for me. But I think I'm ready to be a little selfish, at least where Nick is concerned."

Noelle wagged her finger at her. "Just watch out when the season starts. Some of those groupies are downright treacherous."

Holly's stomach sank, thinking about the beautiful women who would throw themselves at Nick.

"I know that look. You have nothing to worry about. From what I've seen, Nick only has eyes for you."

"This is all really new for me and I get scared sometimes."

"I get it. It's like it's too good to be true."

Holly exhaled. "Exactly."

"No one is perfect. Loving someone means accepting both the good and the bad. None of us are perfect—we're just doing the best we can."

"Thanks Noelle. I needed to hear that."

LATER, AFTER WORK, THE FIREPLACE CRACKLED AND POPPED while the rain beat down outside of her apartment. Holly watched the flames flicker, thinking about her conversation with Noelle earlier.

She picked up her phone and looked at the text from Nick again. He'd asked if she could take three days off for their next date. Getting the time off wasn't the problem; he was asking her to take off the weekend before Christmas, which she usually did anyway. She always worked on most holidays so that a coworker who did celebrate could have the time off.

She turned the phone over in her hand, her finger hovered over the button for a second before she finally pressed it.

"Hey," Nick answered on the first ring.

"Do you have a minute?"

"For you, I have all the time in the world," he said in a low sexy voice that made her stomach flutter and wish he was there, sitting with her. She wrapped her arm around her middle imagining Nick's arms wrapped tightly around her instead of just hearing his voice over the phone.

"I can take the time off next weekend," she blurted out.

"That's great. I'll pick you up Friday morning. Make sure you pack for snow."

Holly chewed on her lip. "I was just wondering about… well…are we going to be sleeping in the same room?"

As soon as she said it out loud, she threw down the phone

with a frustrated groan. She was a grown woman and a nurse. There was no reason she should be nervous about this.

"Holly?" Nick called out, his voice muffled by the sofa cushions where the phone landed.

She picked up the phone when he called her name again.

"I'm here."

"We're staying in a house that has a few bedrooms and you can choose anyone you want." His voice dropped to a husky tone that made her heart jump. "I have to be honest, I hope you'll consider choosing mine, but the choice is yours, Holly. I'll be happy as long as I get to spend time with you."

She squeezed her eyes shut and blew out a shaky breath. "Thank you."

"I'll see you Friday."

"Bye, Nick."

"Good night, Holly."

A couple of days later, she stared into her overnight bag. Her nerves threatened to make her abandon the whole idea of going away with Nick.

She crossed her arms and eyed the contents. She'd packed everything she needed for the long weekend, except for two important things. Nothing she owned resembled a nightgown, let alone anything sexy. To her surprise she wanted to be sexy. She wanted to feel beautiful and confident this weekend. She didn't have a lot of time before Nick was due to arrive, but she needed to make the time for this. Grabbing her car keys and her handbag Holly headed out.

"Come on, put your big girl panties on," she muttered to herself, standing in front of the condom display at the drugstore fifteen minutes later. It wasn't a matter of not being sure if she wanted to take the next step with Nick, but more the case of not having a clue what she should buy. *Why* did there have to be so many choices and sizes?

She pulled out her phone and called the one person she could think of who would give her his honest opinion.

"Thanh, I need your advice."

She explained she was shopping for condoms and after a pause, he said, "Since you don't know about the size of his… package, go for something basic. Get something you'll be comfortable using and will make the experience good for you. This is a two-way street, remember."

Thanh stayed on the phone with her reading through the options until her selection was added to her shopping basket. She thanked him and took a deep breath. One thing off her list and one to go.

Thanh's advice stayed with her when she made her next stop at the lingerie store. She ignored the lacy thongs and anything with bows, opting for a simple black silk camisole and short set instead. She needed something that she would feel comfortable in and would make her feel confident.

She passed by a stationery store on her way back to her car and paused, looking at the display of holiday cards in the window. A card with a snowy Seattle skyline caught her eye and she went in. She added a handful of cards to her purchases and headed home.

There was a knock on her door just as she zipped her overnight bag closed.

Nick stood on her doorstep with a smile that sent her pulse racing.

"Ready to go?" he asked after giving her a quick kiss.

She looked into his eyes, seeing his own excitement in their depths and her nerves settled. Nick would take care of her, she trusted him and knew without a doubt that she was ready to take the next step with him.

CHAPTER 8

Nick took her hands in his and brushed over her knuckles with his thumb. "Thank you for coming away with me this weekend. Your trust means everything to me."

Her cheeks tinged with pink and she dropped her gaze.

"I'm not great with trusting people."

He leaned forward. "I know. It's one of the many things I like about you. Knowing I've gotten you to trust me even just a little makes me feel like I'm a better man."

He dropped a quick kiss on her forehead before he picked up her bag and put it in the back of the car.

Holly looked at the sleek black SUV parked next to her little Jetta station wagon. "Is this new?"

"It is. I decided I needed something more practical than a Porsche for the Pacific Northwest winters."

He opened the door for her and she inhaled the new-car smell as she sank into the plush leather seat.

Nick got in and the engine roared to life. They crossed the I-90 bridge heading east, the city quickly turning into lush forest. The steady rain they had been driving through became mixed with snow and as they climbed higher through the mountains, they drove through a flurry of large fat flakes.

They made it over the pass without having to put chains on and continued on for another hour, following the directions he'd programmed into the GPS, until they pulled off onto a side road and they reached another turnoff with a closed gate. Nick lowered his window and punched in the code to open it. They made their way down a long driveway until they came to a large log cabin by the side of a small lake.

"It's beautiful," Holly exclaimed, gazing at the impressive structure that was more of a house than a cabin.

There were large two-story windows that faced the lake and a massive deck making use of the view. Inside, there was a great room with an open kitchen and an enormous fireplace. Nick knew it was as cozy inside as it looked on the outside.

"Let's get everything unloaded and then we can explore."

"This place is amazing," Holly said, looking around as she got out of the SUV. "How did you find it?"

"It belongs to Dane Prescott."

"I've met him a few times when he's come to the hospital. He's one of the owners of the Emeralds, isn't he?"

"He is. Nice guy. He and Hugh are old friends, so the three of us have hung out a few times." He held his hand out to her. "Come on, let's look around."

Together, they toured the house, Holly's eyes wide. One side of the main room had a huge master suite with a fireplace and a tub in the adjoining bathroom that could easily fit the two of them. There were two smaller bedrooms on the other side of the cabin. The entire cabin was decorated in earth tones with navy blue and dark green accents that complimented the log walls.

"Well, what do you think?"

"It's incredible. I can't believe he's letting us stay here."

Nick nodded. "Dane said he hasn't used it since he bought it. He was happy to have someone come and stay."

"I don't understand how he could have something so beautiful and just let it sit here empty."

"I know," he said. "If I had a place like this, I would want to be here all the time."

"Me too," she sighed, a dreamy look in her eyes.

"There's a place where we can rent cross-country skis not too far from here if we want."

"That would be fun."

"Are you hungry? I'm starving. How about we have some lunch?"

Nick was thankful to Dane for making sure the kitchen was fully stocked before they had arrived. He opened the refrigerator and spied a container of stew that just needed to be warmed up, and buttery-looking biscuits to go along with it.

Before long, they were sitting at the marble-topped kitchen island, watching the snow fall on the water while they ate.

"Are you looking forward to seeing your family for Christmas?" Holly finally asked.

"I am, though it's become more difficult for us to get together these days. Between my sisters' schedules and Jason's touring, I don't know when we'll all be able to see each other again after Christmas."

Holly dipped her biscuit into the stew. "I can't believe your brother is a famous singer now. I watched him on the Grammys. It was so surreal, seeing him on the stage with all those other celebrities. I remember him when he was a kid!"

"My sisters are still mad that he didn't take all of them as his dates," he said with a chuckle.

Holly's lips twitched with amusement.

The sky was already growing darker when they finished lunch and he was eager to show Holly his next surprise. As soon as they cleaned up, he impulsively pulled her into his arms and kissed her.

His desire flared to life, but he tamed it down. He told her he wouldn't push and he meant to keep that promise. As much as he wanted to pursue the physical side of their relationship, he would wait until Holly was ready. He'd finally met a woman worth waiting for.

Her face was flushed and her lips were dark pink when he pulled away. As tempted as he was to keep her in his arms, he was excited to share his surprise for Holly.

"The cabin isn't the date," he told her. "There's more." He led her over to the sofa and had her sit down. "Wait right here for just a minute."

Nick went out to his car and pulled out the packages he'd hidden under a blanket in the back seat. He set the pile of packages wrapped in dark blue paper with tiny gold stars in front of her.

Her gaze flickered in confusion between the packages and him.

"It's part of the date. I promise. Go ahead."

The way she had before, she carefully pulled away the paper from the first box, folded it and set it aside, before opening it. She pulled out a deep plum-colored parka and ran her hand over the soft trim on the hood.

"It's faux fur and I had to guess the size. I hope it's okay."

"It's beautiful, but I already have a coat, Nick," she said.

"I just wanted to make sure you'd be warm enough."

She lifted out the matching snow pants and shook her head. "I don't understand. Are we going skiing?"

"Keep going," he said, gesturing to the next box.

She unwrapped the next box and found snow boots and socks. When she got to the last package, he held his breath as she unwrapped to see the matching snowshoes.

She looked at him, her forehead wrinkled. "Snowshoeing?"

"You can change in the master bedroom. I'll change in one of the other rooms," he offered.

She picked up the boxes and hesitated for just a minute, her eyes filled with wariness.

"Trust me, Holly. It's going to be fun, I promise," he reassured her.

She nodded and hurried into the master bedroom. Nick slipped into the nearest other bedroom and changed quickly into his own gear before he grabbed the snowshoes he'd purchased for himself.

Holly came out just as he walked back into the main room. The ends of two short braids were sticking out from underneath her knit cap. She gave him a little wave with her mitten-covered hands, beaming.

"Ready?"

"I think so."

They stepped out onto the porch and he helped her buckle into her snowshoes before putting on his own.

"Everything fit okay?" he asked. "I asked Noelle for help with the sizes and Thanh told me you like purple."

"Everything is perfect, thank you."

They made their way down the stairs and took a few tentative steps through the deep powdery snow. Holly grinned at him, her eyes sparkling in the moonlight.

He pulled out two headlamps and handed her one. "We aren't going too far, but I thought these would be good to have." He quickly showed her how to use them, helping her slip hers over her cap. Together, they snapped them on.

The lights bounced off of the trees and snowdrifts as their feet made steady crunching sounds in the deep snow. He led her down toward the lake and around the edge until they reached a large clearing.

"Look up," he said in a hushed voice. The stars sparkled and swirled into the Milky Way in the clear night sky.

As he watched, she gazed up with awe.

"It reminds me of a dress I saw an actress wear on the red carpet. Rhinestones on midnight blue velvet. It's amazing."

"My grandparents have a beach house back in Florida. My grandpa always kept a telescope on the porch and when my brother and sisters and I were little we would spend hours stargazing and learning about the constellations with him."

Holly squinted up at the sky. "I only know about the Big Dipper."

"Here," He wrapped his arm around her and lifted her hand to the sky. "there's the Big Dipper, and there's the Little Dipper. If you follow the star at the end of the tail on the Little Dipper, it will lead you to Pegasus," he said, tracing out the figures with their hands joined.

He let go of her hand and turned to face her.

"Happy winter solstice, Holly."

Once again, he took out a small package from his pocket.

She pulled off her mittens and unwrapped the small box. Her gasp came out as a tiny puff when she saw the tiny diamond charm in the shape of the Big Dipper, just like the stars above them. He took his gloves off and reached to pull out the necklace she wore with the airplane and strawberry charm from under her sweater and coat, undoing the clasp and adding the Big Dipper charm to the other two before putting it back around her neck again. Her fingers shook when she reached up to caress the charms on her neck.

He took her hands in his and blew warm air on them before she slipped them back into her mittens.

She started to put her arms around his neck, but her snowshoes tangled with his and they both tumbled into the snow, laughing.

Nick cupped the back of her neck and pulled her down for a kiss that created a spark of warmth in the frosty night air.

The cold drove him to end the kiss sooner than he would have liked, since he was losing sensation in his face. He glanced at Holly, watching her take in the winter wonderland that surrounded them. He'd never put so much thought into planning dates for anyone, but then he'd never met someone who made him want to before.

Nick pictured coming back here in the summer with Holly and going to hikes or swimming in the lake. Four dates would not be enough for all the things he wanted to share with her.

CHAPTER 9

The tiny diamonds glinted in the mirror just like the stars she'd been looking up at earlier. Holly traced the pattern of the Big Dipper charm on the necklace. They'd come in from snowshoeing and now she stood in front of the mirror in the master bathroom. She'd showered and changed into the black camisole set, and her hair had dried into soft waves that brushed against her collar bone. She looked at her eyes reflected in the mirror and didn't see any uncertainty, only excitement and…love. Her nerves had settled, she had fallen in love with Nick, and she trusted him. That made her even more confident with her decision, she wanted this moment and she wanted it to be with Nick.

Making love to Nick didn't scare her. Opening the door to her heart did. She'd kept it closed for so long.

Holly slipped on the matching robe, and at the last second, she untied the robe, letting the soft folds caress her skin. She walked out to the bedroom room where Nick stood in front of the large window, looking out at the forest and the lake below. The desire in his eyes when he saw her took away any lingering doubts that she may have had. She didn't know how it had happened. He had a carefree way about him that reminded her of a video she once saw of cliff divers. Nick threw himself into life the way the divers hurtled themselves off the cliff into the ocean below. She was ready to take the jump into life with this man she'd fallen in love with.

She moved to his side and he wrapped his arm around her waist, drawing her close.

"It's like we're in our own snow globe, our own little bubble of peace and quiet here," she whispered.

On the way back from their stargazing she told him she wanted him to share a room with her that night. He'd kissed her, his eyes filled with a mixture of passion and concern. She saw it again now as he caressed her face.

"Are you sure you want me to stay?" he asked again. His voice was a low seductive whisper that caressed her just as thoroughly as his hands.

She lifted herself up on her toes. Her mouth hovered just below his. "I'm absolutely sure."

The minute her lips pressed against his, a fire ignited between them. Heat flared as he deepened the kiss. His arms banded around her as his mouth devoured hers.

She stayed locked in his embrace as they stumbled toward the bed, trusting him to guide her safely. They toppled onto the mattress and he began to kiss each part of her body, and she matched each of his caresses with one of her own. Holly slid her hands over his muscles, learning every plane and contour. A sigh of longing mixed with pleasure escaped her when he brushed against the sensitive places on her body. She wanted him to linger but she needed more. His hands skimmed over her body, pausing only to remove her clothes. For the first time she knew what it meant to be loved, and cherished.

. . .

Later, after they'd raided the refrigerator and Dane's extensive wine cellar, they were once again snuggled under the covers. The falling snow enveloped them in their own personal snow globe.

"Are you sure you're okay?" he asked, his eyes searching hers.

She smiled at the tenderness in his gaze. "I'm the best I've ever been."

He nuzzled her neck, placing a tender kiss behind her ear, sending another shiver of desire through her. Nick propped himself up on one hand while he drew a line in the valley between her breasts.

"I hate that I have to leave you for the rest of the holidays."

Shaking her head, she turned to face him and took his face in her hands. "You should never feel bad about spending time with your family, Nick."

"I wish you could come with me."

Holly's stomach dipped. The idea of spending Christmas with a big family was something she'd always fantasized about, and yet it scared her.

"I don't know if I could face all the Andersons at once. If I remember, your family can be…overwhelming."

Nick chuckled. "We can be a bit much."

"Besides, if you go away you get to come back. And you know what they say…" Her mouth curled into a shy smile. "Absence makes the heart grow fonder."

His eyes filled with a lustful gleam. "I think we'd better practice for our reunion."

They talked and laughed and made love through the night and into the next day. When the weekend ended, Holly was sad to say good-bye to the cabin in the woods. She smiled softly, fingering the charms on the necklace Nick had given to her as they drove down the mountain and back to civilization and reality.

The days leading up to Nick's departure flew by, and before she was ready, it was the night before Nick left to see his family.

She intertwined her fingers with his as they sat in front of the fireplace at her apartment. "I'm going to miss you," she said.

"I'll call and text every day."

She got up and retrieved the holiday cards she'd made out and handed them to him. "These are for your family."

He shuffled through all of them and looked at her. "This is really nice of you. Thank you."

"Promise you won't open yours until Christmas."

"I promise. I have something for you, it won't be ready until tomorrow morning before I leave."

Holly gave him a kiss. "I don't need presents. I just need you to have a safe trip and think of me when I'm away."

"That I can do."

He gave her one last lingering kiss before he left for the night.

Holly wrapped her arms around herself and wandered back over to sit in front of the fire. It had been a long time since she'd felt the sense of loss she felt now. She'd opened a door to her heart that she couldn't close again—and she didn't want to.

She'd fallen in love with Nick in three dates. They still had one more, and no matter what Nick had planned or what holiday they were going to share, she knew that the date would end with her telling Nick that she loved him.

"Earth to Holly," Thanh called out, waving his hand in front of her face.

She blinked. "What?"

The buzz of the other conversations happening in the bar returned as Holly became aware of her surroundings again. Nick was busy doing some last-minute holiday shopping before his flight the next morning so she was on her own that evening. Her friends had convinced her to come out for a drink after work, but she knew what they really wanted to do was find out what was going on with Nick. She didn't mind. In fact, having friends who cared about her warmed her heart.

Noelle gave her a knowing smile. "Sorry," Holly muttered, her cheek warming.

"I remember being like that when I fell in love with Milo," Thanh said with a smile.

"I didn't say anything about love," Holly exclaimed.

"But things are going well, right?" Noelle asked.

"They are." Holly fingered the charms on her necklace. "I just wish… Nick is so generous, and I just hope he knows that I don't expect to get gifts from him all the time. Spending time together is better than anything he could give me. I just wish…I knew if he felt the same way."

Thanh gave her a nod. "That's understandable. Have you said anything to him about it?"

"No, not yet. I need to. I just… We've been having so much fun, I don't want to do anything to…"

"Break the spell?" Noelle asked.

Holly took a deep breath and nodded.

"You aren't Cinderella, and this isn't a fairy tale. Talk to him. If he cares about you, he'll understand," Thanh said.

CHAPTER 10

Nick straightened the bow on the gift and stood back to make sure it looked perfect before he went to get Holly. Glancing at his watch he let out a frustrated sigh. There wasn't much time before he needed to get to the airport and catch his flight. He'd sacrificed spending the night with her to get her gift ready. He missed the feel of her skin against his already, but it would be worth it when he got to see the look on her face.

"No peeking and don't open your eyes until I tell you to," Nick said as he carefully led Holly down the stairs from her apartment. He carefully positioned her and took the blindfold off. "Ready?"

She smiled and nodded, her eyes still closed. "I'm ready."

He dropped a quick kiss on her forehead. "One. Two. Three. Open your eyes."

Holly's eyes flew open. She looked at the brand-new shiny red SUV with a huge gold bow on the top. He opened the back to reveal the cargo space, filled with wrapped presents.

"I know you don't celebrate Christmas, but that doesn't mean that I can't. Merry Christmas, Holly."

Instead of the excitement and joy he expected to see, he only saw anger blazing in the depths of Holly's amber eyes.

Her gaze swiveled from the car back to him, with wide eyes.

"What in the world are you thinking? This is a fricking car, Nick."

"Surprise," he said, not feeling nearly as jubilant as he did just a minute ago.

"The charms, and the snowshoeing equipment, were lovely gifts. But even those were too extravagant."

"I was just trying to show you how much our time together meant to me. Maybe the car was a little over the top, but I just wanted to do this for you to show that you don't have to hate Christmas."

"Is this why you think I don't like Christmas, because I didn't get presents?"

His brow wrinkled in confusion. He thought now that they were together she would loosen up and wouldn't be so hesitant to enjoy the lifestyle he could provide for her. Why couldn't she see that he just wanted to take care of her?

"I just thought… I wanted to make up for all the years you didn't get anything."

She took a deep, shuddering breath. "I can't believe you think I'm that shallow. You said you weren't going to be that guy. You said you understood. I don't need someone to swoop in and shower me with gifts. You can't make up for what I didn't have growing up, with gifts."

"I don't think you're shallow at all," he answered desperately. "You're one of the most down to earth and honest people I've ever met and that's why I… I've fallen in love with you."

He reached out to wipe away the tear that slowly fell down her cheek, but she pulled away, shaking her head.

Oh, crap.

"You don't love me. If you did, you would know what Christmas means to me. I don't want a new car, Nick. Do you know why I love my car?" She pointed at her little silver Jetta wagon. "Because I earned it. I earned every penny and it was the first brand-new thing I ever bought myself. You throw your money around like it means something and you don't appreciate what really matters. I can't…" Her voice broke.

Tears tracked down her face, but she straightened and looked him in the eye. "I can't be with someone who doesn't understand that love and the holidays aren't about things." She gently pushed him back. "Go home, Nick. Go see your family."

With that, she turned and walked away, leaving Nick stunned. He started to follow her and stopped. He knew she wasn't going to let him in.

Looking at the car filled with presents his heart sank. He'd been so confident that he could give Holly the best Christmas ever and instead he'd lost her.

His phone vibrated.

"Hey, Holly's on the phone and she's pretty upset," Hugh said in a grim voice.

"I messed up," Nick blurted out.

"It sounds like it. I'm just calling to see if there's anything I can do to help."

"No, I'll take care of the gifts when I get back. I have a flight to catch."

"I can take care of that for you and don't worry about Holly. Noelle and I will check in on her while you're gone."

Nick pinched the bridge of his nose. "Thanks, man. I appreciate that. I'll call you when I get home and we can work out the details. Maybe you can find somewhere to donate the gifts. And I'll call the dealership to have the car picked up.

There was a beat of silence. "I can't believe you bought her a car."

"Yeah, I…I made a mistake."

Nick hung up and stared up at her apartment. He wanted to go to her, but he wasn't sure what to say. A second later Poornima came out of the house and rushed toward Holly's apartment, throwing him an angry glance as she went by.

He didn't think about himself as being careless with his money. He was generous because he could be and he'd always given extravagant gifts to his family and friends. What was wrong with that?

Two days later he was sitting on the couch in his parents' family room, scrolling through the unanswered texts he'd sent Holly.

"Stop moping, Nick."

His brother flopped down on the couch next to him. Holly hadn't answered any of his texts or phone calls since he left, and Nick was both frustrated and worried. The family had just finished their traditional family dinner and he was lounging on the couch, pretending to give a damn about the football game blaring on TV when all he could think about was Holly. He knew she was working on Christmas Eve, and he hated the idea of her coming home to an empty apartment at the end of her shift.

"I'm not moping, I'm thinking."

Jason rolled his eyes.

Okay, so maybe he was moping. He missed Holly and he was mad at himself for pushing too hard.

"Nick, will you come help me, please?" his mother called.

He pulled himself up and trudged toward the kitchen.

His mother threw a towel at him. "I'll wash, you dry."

"Mom, we have a dishwasher."

"You know the crystal can't go in the dishwasher."

He nodded. He knew. "It was a wonderful Christmas dinner. Thanks, Mom."

"I'm surprised you tasted any of it, you were so busy sulking."

"Why does everyone keep saying I'm sulking?"

"Because you are," his dad said, walking into the kitchen.

"George, Nick and I are talking, and you will not sneak another piece of pie."

"I wasn't trying to sneak another—"

His mother's raised eyebrow had his father turning right around and heading out of the room. It reminded Nick of how Holly looked at him when she was frustrated with him.

He sighed and started wiping the glass his mother handed him.

"He's right, though. You've been moody ever since you got here," she said quietly.

"I screwed up," he confessed.

"Let me guess. You went too fast and overwhelmed her."

He dropped his dishtowel and leaned against the sink. "How did you know?"

"Sweetheart. You are generous and loving to a fault, and you're a fixer." She gave him a wistful smile. "You get that from me."

"I just wanted her to have what I had growing up. I hated knowing that she woke up every Christmas without a bunch of presents under the tree."

His mother frowned at him. "Is that what you think matters? Oh, Nick." She sighed, shaking her head. "Your heart was in the right place, but you got the message mixed up. If you grew up the way Holly did, what would matter: more presents or having a family?"

Holly's last words came back to him. *Go home to your family.*

Family.

No gift could replace a family. That was what Holly missed every Christmas, a family of her own.

"Shit," he muttered.

Nick threw the dishtowel down on the counter and leaned against the counter, his head bowed.

His embarrassment quickly turned into anger. How could he have been so blind? He remembered all the times she mentioned how much he'd spent on their dates. Even though they had fun, her smile was bigger and her eyes sparkled brighter when they were doing the simplest things, and it was because they were doing them together.

"You look like you might be having an epiphany," his mom said, watching him with an amused gleam in her eye.

"I don't think she'll forgive me."

"If you apologize the right way without making a big grand gesture, I think she will. I've always liked that girl. I'd be thrilled to welcome her as a daughter-in-law someday," she said with a sly smile.

"Nick's getting married?" his youngest sister Beth squealed as she walked into the kitchen.

"To who?" Amanda, the middle of his three sisters, asked.

His oldest sister, Melissa, followed the other two into the kitchen.

"I'm not getting married and it's none of your business," he growled.

"Girls, leave your brother alone." His mother shooed them out of the kitchen.

"I'm sorry, Mom."

"I'm not the one you need to apologize to. How about you stop texting and calling for a few days and give her some space?"

"When I gave her the car I told her I loved her," he said.

His mother slapped her forehead. "Oh Nick. You bought her a car?"

"And I may have filled it with presents," he mumbled.

She threw a dishtowel at him. "Of all the… I can't believe you thought that was a good idea. Let me guess. You're worried because she didn't respond when you told her you loved her."

He ducked his head. It all seemed so obviously dumb in hindsight.

"Please. I'm begging you, please, don't read the 'Lovers are patient' quote," he said when his mother started for her desk drawer.

Anytime any of the Anderson kids had trouble with their love life, their mother pulled out a tattered and worn copy of a saying from the poet Rumi. Too late.

He sighed while she held up the paper and read aloud.

" 'Patience is not sitting and waiting, it is foreseeing. It is looking at the thorn and seeing the rose, looking at the night and seeing the day. Lovers are patient and know that the moon needs time to become full.' Give her time, Nick."

He went over and pulled his mom into a hug. "Merry Christmas, Mom."

She pulled back and put her hands on his cheeks. "Merry Christmas, son."

The next morning, Nick and his family opened the cards Holly had sent with him. As he watched, tears streamed down his mother's face.

"I can't believe she remembered that," Melissa said looking down at the card.

"What did she write?" he asked.

"She wrote a memory. About a time she saw me with Beth and Amanda at the park and how she admired what a good big sister she thought I was."

Nick opened his card and the words she'd written to him blurred as he blinked back his own tears. She wrote how she remembered watching him play soccer in high school and how she had silently cheered him on. About how she would pretend that every goal he scored was just for her. And then she wrote how those memories and the new ones they were making together were the most precious gift he could ever give her.

Holly had written one memory she had of each member of his family, a story from school or a memory of watching his youngest sister learning how to ride her bike.

Holly hadn't given them things; she had given them memories.

CHAPTER 11

"How about you come out on the boat with Hugh and me for New Year's?" Noelle offered.

Holly sighed and shook her head. The last thing she wanted to be was a third wheel on what she was sure Hugh was planning on being a romantic weekend.

"Thanks, but I'm working on New Year's."

"I'm sorry about what happened with Nick, but promise me you won't just hide yourself away in this hospital," Noelle said.

"I'll try." Holly gave her a small smile.

It was a quiet night, at least. Making her rounds, she took extra time with the two patients who were in foster care. Holly always put aside as much extra time as she could with the kids who didn't have a family member who could be with them.

She listened as they excitedly showed off the gifts they had received from Santa. They had no idea that they were showing off the gifts she had secretly purchased for them. They weren't over-the-top gifts like what Nick had done.

Holly liked to give the children books or a journal with a nice pen. Just like she had been, these were kids who understood that no gift could replace having a family.

Holly had finished up with her last patient and headed back to her station when she heard Nick's voice down the hallway, calling her name.

She winced when her clogs squeaked while she turned around and made her way quickly down the hallway. She ducked into the supply closet and blew out a shaky breath.

The last week without Nick had been terrible. She had missed him so much, but she was still so disappointed in him. When his texts and phone calls had stopped, she felt a pang of regret for having been so stubborn.

Her phone rang and she fumbled, trying to get it out of her pocket and quickly silence it. Then she saw the name on the caller ID.

Nick.

She was still debating answering when the ringing stopped. But she jumped when he called again. Before she could change her mind, she answered.

"Hello?"

"Hi, Holly. Could you please come out of the supply closet?"

She closed her eyes and muttered a silent oath. She really needed to learn that hiding in supply closets didn't work.

"Please don't hang up," he said, when she opened the door a crack to peek out.

He looked terrible. There were dark circles under his eyes and his hair looked like he'd run his hands through it more than once.

"Holly I'm sorry I went overboard and I didn't take your feelings into consideration." He gripped the phone tighter pressing it to his ear. "I can be impatient and I was so excited about what I could give you I didn't think about what you would actually *want*. I know now that presents aren't what matters. Being with people you love and care about is the best gift, no matter what holiday you celebrate. I don't care if you don't like Christmas. The only thing that matters is that you know, I like you."

Nick's face became blurry and she blinked to clear the image and keep her tears at bay. "That's all I've ever wanted, to be surrounded by people I love," she said, her voice thick, into her phone. They were still both on their phones, even as they were looking at each other. "Things don't matter if you don't have people you love to share them with."

"Wait." He held up his hand when she started to hang up. "There's one more thing I wanted to say." He gave her a half smile. "Happy National Call a Friend Day. I'm glad that I got to become friends with you and I know you might not be ready to say it back but I… I love you."

Her phone clattered to the floor. She threw herself into his arms, and held his face in her hands. "I love you, Nick."

His lips came down on hers, and everything she'd ever hoped love could be, she felt in that kiss.

"When do you get off work?" he asked as he peppered her face with kisses.

"Not for another couple of hours."

He sealed his mouth over hers for another toe-curling kiss.

"I have kids to visit. I'll be waiting for you when your shift is over."

She nodded and pulled him in for one more embrace before she let go.

Nick was waiting for her at the nurses' station when she was finished. He whisked her out of the hospital and back to her apartment.

Fevered kisses became much more. Each caress and touch became a promise for a future filled with patience and love between them.

Hours later, Holly lay side by side with Nick, happy and breathing hard. She ran her hand over his beard. "I missed you so much."

"Just about every single member of my family told me to stop moping. And then when they read your cards they all took turns telling me what an idiot I was," he confessed.

"I'm sorry if I ruined your Christmas."

"You didn't, I did. Once I figured out what an ass I'd made of myself, I was so worried that you wouldn't forgive me. I was supposed to stay until New Year's, but my folks made me come back early because they couldn't stand seeing me so sad. Plus, my mother kept reading that damn Rumi quote," he muttered.

She gave him a knowing smile. " 'Patience is not sitting and waiting, it is foreseeing. It is looking at the thorn and seeing the rose, looking at the night and seeing the day. Lovers are patient and know that the moon needs time to become full.' "

"How did you know that was the quote?"

"Your mom wrote it to me in a letter she gave me when I graduated from high school."

Nick reached up to brush the hair out of her eyes. "I want to spend every full moon with you."

"I love you, Nick," she whispered against his lips.

"I'm looking forward to a whole year of holidays where I get to tell you how much I love you."

"I can't wait."

He gave her a cocky grin. "I'm thinking we should start making up our own holidays."

"What kind of holiday?"

“How about we make tomorrow ‘Stay in Bed and Make Love Day,’ ” he said, waggling his eyebrows.

“That sounds like a perfect holiday and I think there’s nothing wrong with celebrating early.”

With Nick she had found a partner who she could learn and grow with. Not every day would be perfect, but they would celebrate each success or failure together. Love was the best holiday of all.

The End

SUMMER OF NOELLE

AN EMERALD HEARTS NOVELLA

CHAPTER 1

"Nurse Christmas, do you have a pet reindeer?" the little girl asked, looking up at Noelle with a combination of awe and thoughtfulness. Her large light brown eyes were exaggerated without hair to frame her tiny head, and a mask covering her mouth. She studied Noelle's movements warily as she adjusted her catheter port.

Noelle gently patted the little girl's arm as the clear liquid that provided the child's body with lifesaving medication began its journey into her body.

"No, sweetheart, the reindeer need to stay at the North Pole with Santa. It's too warm for them in Seattle during the summer."

The wise little woman nodded solemnly in agreement with her explanation.

The little girl's mother came back into the room with a grateful smile and motioned for Noelle to speak to her out of earshot.

"I'll be back to check on you tomorrow, okay, Zoe?"

"Thank you, Nurse Christmas."

Her first patient on her first day at Seattle Children's

Hospital had called her "Nurse Christmas" when she introduced herself as Noelle, and the name stuck. The irony was, Christmas was her least favorite holiday. She avoided the bleak childhood memories that'd plagued her since a young age. A present in a nicely wrapped package didn't always contain a thoughtful gift. Christmas was supposed to be about gingerbread and colorful lights adorning a majestic tree, not drunken fights that resulted in her being forgotten and alone.

The current season was the one she loved. Summer in Seattle was enchanting. It began in fits and starts with a sunny day here and there. And then, all of a sudden, bright blue sky met lush green mountains with glacier-fed waters, luring more than one person to move to the Pacific Northwest on a whim. Summer in Seattle made up for being called Nurse Christmas all year round.

She met Zoe's mother at the door. She grabbed Noelle's arm, her eyes shining with excitement.

"Dr. Sankar just gave me the news. The new immunotherapy looks like it's working," she said in a hushed whisper.

"That's wonderful news. I'm so happy for you."

Zoe's mother gave her a hug. "Everyone here has been amazing, but you have been so kind to Zoe. I know you try to spend extra time with her, and I'll never be able to thank you enough."

Every nurse at Children's Hospital gave their charges the same amount of care and attention, but they all had patients who touched them in a special way. Zoe had captured a piece of Noelle's heart from the moment she met the sweet, precocious six-year-old.

The first time she came into Zoe's room, she observed, "Nurse Christmas, our skin is the same color. Is your mommy white and your daddy Black like mine?"

She always marveled at how the biracial kids knew she was one of them.

The little girl and her mother had traveled across the state to seek treatment while her father stayed behind to run the family farm. He could only come for visits every couple of weeks. Sadly, such cases weren't unusual. The parking lot at the hospital was peppered with license plates not only from Washington, but from Oregon, Idaho, and Wyoming. Sometimes, the cars arrived with travel trailers attached so families had somewhere to live if their child was admitted for an extended period of time.

She said her goodbyes to Zoe and her mother and then bumped right into the friendly face and laughing light-green eyes of the one person she tried to avoid every week.

Hugh Donovan's face lit up with a smile. "Just the person I was looking for."

She sighed. "The answer is still no."

"But I haven't asked the question yet."

Resting her hand on her hip, she raised an eyebrow. "Are you going to ask me something different this week?"

"No, not exactly. Let's see." He scratched his head, looking at her thoughtfully. "I've asked you out to dinner, lunch, breakfast, coffee, tea…" He listed all the ways he had asked her out since she started working at the hospital six months ago.

The star midfielder for the Seattle Emeralds MLS team smiled at her, his gaze hopeful as always. The hospital would occasionally host a professional athlete or celebrity who would come to visit the kids, but Hugh came every week. Noelle's heart softened for just a moment. She admired his commitment to the young patients at the hospital, but then she reminded herself that she wouldn't date a professional athlete ever again. She'd learned her lesson with her ex-husband. She clasped her hands in front of her and steeled herself.

"The answer is still no, I appreciate you asking," she said politely. She would never be intentionally unkind. "But you should find another girl. I'm sure there are plenty out there who would've said yes to you by now."

He frowned and shook his head. "But none of them are you."

Her heart skipped a beat. She was taller than most women at five-eight, but she still had to lift her head to look him in the eye. She didn't dare.

She wasn't going to pretend Hugh Donovan wasn't a handsome man. More than one nurse had swooned over the ad campaign he did for Nike a few months ago. She wouldn't admit she took a turn sneaking a peek. And the picture of him wearing nothing but a pair of form-fitting athletic shorts in his team colors, looking intently at the camera while holding a soccer ball against his hip was swoon worthy.

He didn't have the bulky muscles of her football player ex-husband. Hugh's arms and legs were sinewy, each muscle well defined. He wore his hair long enough to flop over his forehead and his beard close-cropped. The picture in the magazine didn't capture the streaks of red and dark brown in his hair or the way his eyes reminded her of the moss that covered the trees in the rainforest. He exuded confidence. You had to be to play any sport on an elite level. But he wasn't arrogant, and that's what made her stop and pay a bit more attention when he came to visit the hospital.

There was always compassion in his eyes, the same eyes that were looking at her now, with a determination that made her heart beat a little faster.

A little voice called out of the room, "Nurse Christmas, if you don't like tea, maybe you can go out for ice cream."

Her eyes grew wide, looking like a startled owl, her head swiveled toward the slightly ajar door of her patients room. Zoe's mom poked her head out and lowered her mask to mouth, "Sorry." Her eyes sparkled with amusement.

She heard a soft chuckle next to her and closed her eyes, wishing the floor would open up and swallow her.

"I like vanilla because you can add whatever you want and make it something different every time," he said.

Damn it, he even liked the same flavor of ice cream for the same reason. It was getting harder and harder to come up with excuses to dislike Hugh Donovan. When she opened her eyes, he smiled at her with a hopeful look.

"So, ice cream?" He raised his eyebrows.

Little Zoe's voice rang in her ears. "We'll see," she said.

You'd think she'd agreed to marry him the way he beamed at her. "What time do you get off?"

She shook her head, she felt a moment of panic. "Not today, I'll… I'll let you know when I'm ready."

"And I'll be here when you are."

He was so self-assured. Her ex needed to tear everyone down to build himself up. When Hugh turned his gaze toward her, it wasn't to look for a flaw. There wasn't any censure, just… desire.

"I have to get back to my patients," she said, backing away.

He lifted his hand in a friendly half wave before he turned and walked away.

When she returned to the nurses' station, Thanh, her best friend and co-worker, was waiting for her with his arms crossed and his lips pressed into a thin line.

She frowned. "What?"

"It's time," he said.

"Time for what?" Thanh's husband, Milo, walked up, handing his husband his lunch tote.

Noelle admired the way the two of them cared for one another. With Milo working as an ER doc and Thanh's schedule as a nurse, there were some days their lunch handoff was the only time they would see each other.

Thanh sniffed at the tote. "Black-eyed pea salad?" he asked, with a hopeful expression.

Milo grinned and kissed his husband on the cheek. "With your mother's lemongrass chicken."

Thanh groaned in appreciation. "You are the best husband ever."

"I know," Milo said with a wink. "Now, what is it time for?" His gaze went between Noelle and Thanh.

"It's time for Noelle to give our favorite soccer player a break and go out on a date."

Milo's eyes widened. "Oh, *that* time."

"You're going to take his side, aren't you?" she grumbled.

"I am," Milo said with a nod, "and not just because I'm his husband, but because I'm also your friend. I remember how you were when you first moved to Seattle, the haunted look in your eyes. Thanh and I have seen you blossom over the last few years. We know it wasn't easy. Remember how long it took for you to trust us?" Milo asked with a warm smile. "I want you to be happy. Athletes, actors, and celebrities, some show up because they need good press, but Hugh wants to be here. I've gotten to know him. Thanh and I have met up with him for drinks a few times, and he's ridiculously nice. He treats the people around him with respect and kindness, and not just the kids, but the staff as well. Did you know he made a big donation to the hospital library? And it wasn't just money. The guy consulted with the librarian and went out and bought a thousand dollars' worth of books, and he picked each one out himself."

Thanh nodded in agreement with his husband's words.

"I know he's nice. I've seen the way he is with the kids and how he treats everyone here. I overheard him checking in on Debbie a few weeks ago after she lost a patient and the way he spoke to her was beautiful." She sighed. "But I'm just… not ready."

Milo put his arm around her shoulder. "You're just scared, and there's nothing wrong with that."

Thanh came over and took her hands in his. "When I was a little boy, I took swimming lessons, and on the last day of class, we all got to jump off the high dive. Most of the kids climbed up, looked over the edge, and climbed back down without jumping. When it was my turn, I climbed up and looked over the edge. The water seemed so far away, and I was scared. I started to walk back to the ladder and climb down, and then I stopped. I took a deep breath, turned around, started running, and I jumped," he finished, giving her hands a squeeze. "It's time for you to jump."

She sniffed, blinking back her tears before they could fall. "Thank you," she managed to choke out.

THAT NIGHT, NOELLE BOBBED IN HER KAYAK IN THE WATERS of Lake Washington while she watched the evening commuters slowly inching their way across the 520 bridge, happy she wasn't among them. She'd always wanted to be a nurse; the idea of any kind of job where she had to work in a cubicle never appealed to her. After a brief disastrous turn as a gridiron trophy wife, she achieved her goal and completed the nursing program she'd started in college.

With a new career, new friends, and a new place to live,

she'd done everything she needed to make herself happy, and yet her fear of making the wrong choice again held her back. She got out of an abusive marriage and put a lot of effort into healing. Her ex wanted to appear successful on and off the field, and she was expected to look the part all day, every day. She had to wear the right clothes and say the right things, and if she didn't, the consequences were swift and severe. Her hand shook running it over loose curls. When she first came to Seattle, she'd cut if all off. She vowed she'd never let a man use her hair to punish her again. Taking Krav Maga lessons gave her the strength and confidence to reclaim her crown.

She'd made wonderful friends in Seattle. Dov Koren, her Krav Maga instructor, and his wife, Aviva, had become a second family to her. Her coworker Thanh and his husband, Milo, took her under their wing on day one and taught her how to have fun again. But finding herself interested in a relationship again took her by surprise. Could she risk her everything she'd done to heal for another chance at love?

As she looked out over the expanse of blue sky reflected in the water, she thought about how nice it would be to have someone to share it with. The ink was dry from her divorce, but her heart was still frozen. She rested the paddle across her lap and let her fingers trail in the cool water while her mind drifted to her conversation with Hugh that afternoon.

On his last visit to the hospital, he remembered that one of her co-worker's daughters was starting soccer camp that week, and he'd brought her a signed jersey from one of his NWSL teammates. He was always doing thoughtful things like that, little acts of kindness that most people might not notice, but she did. She trusted Thanh and Milo, and they were right. Hugh was worth taking a risk for.

Craning her neck she watched an eagle make slow circles

in the sky, searching for its evening meal. Another benefit to summer in the Pacific Northwest were the long days. At this time of year, it would be after nine p.m. before the sun set. A summer night on the water was the perfect way to end her day.

The eagle flexed his wings and glided through the warm air. It was time for her to follow his lead and stretch her wings. The next time she saw Hugh, she'd say yes to ice cream.

CHAPTER 2

The automatic doors opened with a quiet hiss, and a blast of air conditioning welcomed Hugh when he walked back into the hospital for his weekly visit.

"Morning, Mr. Donovan. How's the leg feeling?"

The young man at the check-in desk handed him the ID badge that all visitors were required to wear.

"It's much better, Gabe. I think I'll get the all-clear to start rehab next week."

Gabe's eyes lit up. "Maybe you'll be back on the field by the playoffs."

Hugh noted the eagerness in his voice. He was doubtful he would play at all this season, and the idea didn't bother him as much as he thought it would. He'd been playing hard both at his sport and life. It was time to take a break, but he didn't want to disappoint a fan, so he smiled and said, "I'll do my best, but the decision is up to the training staff and the coach."

"I'll keep my fingers crossed." Gabe held up both of his hands.

"Thanks."

He waved and made his way to the bank of elevators. He took one several floors down and walked through the familiar maze of hallways painted with a colorful forest mural to the pediatric oncology wing of the hospital.

He shifted the bag of signed soccer balls, scarves, and Seattle Emeralds blankets he brought with him to give out to the kids he would visit this week. Normally, he wasn't able to come every week during the season, but this year, he wasn't traveling with the team, giving him more time to spend with the kids and the one person he couldn't stop thinking about. Injuries were a part of life for a professional athlete, and he had his fair share. This one was different, the most severe so far, and a reminder that he was getting older and his career wasn't going to last forever. He needed to start making plans for his future, and that included settling down with someone who would make his day brighter with just a smile. A woman who would support his dreams and he could support hers. A partner, a friend, and a lover. Maybe he was being selfish, but he wanted it all.

It was impossible to reign in his excitement. He'd been trying to get Noelle Wright to talk to him since the first time he saw her. He didn't believe in love at first sight—until he met the beautiful, reserved pediatric nurse. He had it pretty easy when it came to dating, or he could, if he were attracted to groupies. Through high school and college, Hugh learned pretty quickly that certain people were always attracted to talent, popularity, and fame. He also figured out that most of those people took what they could get. Noelle was the only person he'd encountered since he became a professional player who seemed to disapprove of him being an athlete.

She was sitting at the nurses' station when he arrived to

pick up the list of patients he would visit that day. Her dark blue scrub bottoms were paired with a top covered in colorful mermaids on a turquoise background that complemented her light brown skin. She glanced up, her amber eyes flickering toward him, and then bowed her head so her hair hid her face.

"Morning, Hugh," her coworker, Thanh, greeted him with a wave.

His gaze darted to where Noelle sat staring at her tablet, avoiding eye contact, though a faint blush spread over her cheeks. He exchanged a look with Thanh, who shrugged.

He cleared his throat. "Good morning, Noelle."

She reached for a piece of paper and handed it to him. "Here's today's list. Make sure you review it carefully."

He set the bag on the floor and rested his elbows on the counter. "Could you take a few minutes to look at it with me?"

She frowned and spun around in her chair. "I have patients I need to check on," she said as she jumped up, pulling her wavy, dark brown hair into a ponytail while she walked away.

Thanh folded his arms and sat back. "If it's any help, she's interested. She's just… scared."

"What's she afraid of?" he muttered, watching her disappear down the hallway.

"She doesn't talk about it much, but her marriage was a train wreck. That guy…" Milo pressed his lips together and shook his head. "I hope the steroids make his dick fall off someday," he spat out.

Nodding, he wished there was something he could do to help speed up the process. The thought of anyone hurting Noelle made his blood boil.

"She's still a little gun-shy. Be patient. She'll come

around when she's ready, and hey, Milo and I are rooting for you." Thanh thumped him on the back.

"Thanks, man. I appreciate it."

"By the way, thanks again for the tickets to the last home game. Those seats were awesome. Milo's voice is still hoarse from all the yelling."

Thanh's husband was a big Emeralds fan, and Hugh was happy to pass on tickets for a game when he could. He'd made the same offer to Noelle, but she always turned him down.

"There's gotta be something," he muttered.

Thanh leaned forward, his eyes darting back and forth to make sure they weren't overheard. "She likes water. She goes kayaking on Lake Washington after work."

His eyebrows shot up. "I can work with that," he said with a grin.

WHEN HE WAS FINISHED WITH HIS VISIT, NOELLE CALLED OUT to him as he walked past her station.

"Hugh?" Her voice carried a slight tremor as she stood next to the desk, twisting her hands in front of her. "About that ice cream. I can go… I mean, if you still want to," she said, her gaze darting to where Thanh stood by, nodding his encouragement.

He tried to tamp down his enthusiasm. He didn't want to ruin his chance by coming across as too eager. "Great."

Thanh beamed at the two of them and rubbed his hands together. "Good. This is good."

She bowed her head, trying to a shy smile.

"You're supposed to ask what time works for her." Thanh gestured between Hugh and Noelle.

"Okay, I've got it," he said with a pointed look at him.

Thanh backed away, holding his hands up. "Just trying to help."

Once Thanh was out of earshot, Noelle cleared her throat. "I can meet you after my shift tomorrow. I get off at three, if that works for you."

"That sounds perfect."

CHAPTER 3

That evening, Hugh sat on the deck of his house overlooking Lake Washington. He watched a kayaker paddle past cleaving the evening water, imagining it was Noelle. He heard the click of the gate in the fence that separated his property from the house next door, and his neighbor climbed the stairway up to his deck, dropping into a chair next to him. He reached down and handed his friend a beer.

Dane Prescott took a long swig and stared out at the water.

"Long day?" Hugh asked.

"You know, when I founded PresTec in college, I never thought I'd end up spending all my time in board meetings and putting out fires instead of coding."

"Better you than me." Hugh saluted him with his beer.

They drank in silence for a while before Dane asked, "Do you think you're going to be in good shape for next season?"

"Mentally, yes, but…" Hugh reached down to rub his leg. "I got lucky. A ligament injury could have been a career ender. It's made me think about the future. The reality is my body won't take another major hit, and I want to finish my career while I'm still healthy."

"As part owner of the team, that's not what I was hoping to hear, but as your friend, I understand. You know I'll support whatever decision you make."

He blinked and cleared his throat. "Thanks. That means a lot to me to have you say that."

"Maybe your nurse can help you out with physical therapy." Dane waggled his eyebrows.

"She's not my nurse—at least, not yet."

"You know, my sister has a friend…"

He held up his hand. "Stop. The last time I let you set me up with one of your sister's friends, I had to hear about how she was having a hard time finding someone who would make matching outfits for her and her chihuahua."

"Sorry." Dane snorted a laugh.

His best friend meant well, but his last few attempts at setting Hugh up had been disastrous. He didn't bother to add that once he met Noelle, he compared every other woman to her.

He would never forget the first time he saw her at the hospital. He'd been finishing up one of his visits when Thanh introduced him to the new nurse who would be working with him. He was used to people being excited to meet him, so he was thrown off when she gave his hand the briefest shake and avoided eye contact. When she finally met his gaze, those light brown eyes were hesitant, but he caught the slight spark of interest. Her dusky pink lips turned down, and she excused herself, practically running away. It took weeks of patience before she stopped being skittish around him. Each smile had been hard won, but every time that dimple appeared and her eyes lit up, he knew it was worth the effort.

He pinched the bridge of his nose. "Don't forget the one

before that who came to the date with a stack of bridal magazines."

"Dude," Dane said, rolling his eyes, "I owe you a case of wine for that one."

"No more blind dates."

Dane cocked his head, studying him. "So it's the nurse, is it?"

"It is."

"I hope it works out for you."

"You and me both," he sighed.

Dane downed the rest of his beer and stood. "I've got to get back. I promised Jamie two bedtime stories to make up for the one I missed last night."

"Give him a good-night hug from his Uncle Hugh."

Dane nodded and headed back toward the other side of the fence, leaving him alone with his thoughts. He tried to tamp down his excitement for his date the next night. It wasn't even a date, just ice cream, but it was a start. It had taken six months to reach this point, and he wasn't going to take it for granted. Now wasn't the time to get cocky.

He scanned the lake, looking for the kayak he spotted earlier, but it was long gone. He went up and rested his elbows on the deck railing, taking in the view of Mt. Rainier, which he would never get tired of. It had taken a long time to reach a point in his life where he was ready for the life his friend Dane had, with a wife and child to enjoy nights like this with him. He should have been more upset about missing the season than he was, but in a way, he was thankful for the injury. It forced him to slow down and take stock of what was important to him—family, friends, and a partner in life who saw him as more than the sport he played. Noelle could be that person, and he hoped this would be the summer he finally got the chance to find out.

CHAPTER 4

Noelle looked up at the menu board for Annie Elliot's Homemade Ice Cream, feeling silly because with all the choices, she knew she would still pick vanilla, and feeling self-conscious because she was with Hugh. *This isn't a date, it's just ice cream,* she reminded herself for the hundredth time since she finally agreed to meet him after her shift the next week when he came to the hospital.

"Do you know what you want?" Hugh stood beside her, looking up at the menu with her.

"I should probably order something more exciting with all of these options, but I'll have the double cream vanilla."

He nodded to the server. "Two double cream vanillas, please."

"Mister Donovan." A little boy tugged on Hugh's shirt. "Can I please get your autograph?" He held out a piece of paper and a pen.

He took the pen from the boy and eyed his Seattle Emerald T-shirt. He turned back to the server and asked, "Excuse me, do you have a permanent marker?"

The server smiled and handed him a black marker. He knelt down and gently turned the boy so his back was to him. The little boy craned his neck, trying to look over his shoulder with wide eyes to watch Hugh sign his shirt. His parents stood by, the father taking pictures with his phone while the mother beamed and smiled. She took the cones from the server and paid for the ice cream while Hugh spent a few more minutes asking the little boy what position he played and giving him a few words of encouragement before sending him on his way.

He handed the pen back to the server and pulled out his wallet.

She shook her head and pointed to Noelle. "She took care of it."

Hugh turned to her. "This was supposed to be my treat."

"I don't mind." She shrugged. "You were busy."

"Thanks for understanding."

She did understand, in a way most people wouldn't. Her past experience made her appreciate the extra effort he took with the little boy even more. Her ex wouldn't have shown the same kindness and patience that Hugh just had.

They wandered through the outdoor mall with their cones, eventually stopping at a shady seating area.

"So what made you come to Seattle?" he asked between bites.

"There was a movie, *Singles*, set in Seattle. I saw it on TV when I was in junior high, and I fell in love with the idea of living here one day."

"Does that mean you're a Pearl Jam fan?"

"It's a requirement if you live in Seattle. But Soundgarden will always have a special place in my heart."

"You've only been here for six months. Where did you live before you came here?" Hugh asked.

She licked the frozen mixture of cream and sugar, appreciating how something so simple could taste so good. "Life happened," she finally said. "I let go of the dream of coming here for a different one, and it turned out to be a mistake. Luckily, I figured it out in time. I've been here for over a year, actually. I had to spend a semester finishing my nursing degree, and then I was lucky enough to get a job at Children's."

"I'm really glad you did," his gaze held hers just long enough for her to feel the heat rise in her cheeks.

"What about you? Were you disappointed when you were traded to Seattle?"

"I was hoping to play for San Diego so I could be close to my parents, but I've loved playing for the Emeralds. I've been thinking that I'd like to finish my career playing for the Emeralds and retire here."

"Do you know what you're going to do when you're not playing anymore?"

Hugh finished off his cone and dusted his hands on his pants. Leaning forward he rested his arms on his thighs. "I'd like to coach if I can." He paused and waved to the little boy who had asked for his autograph when he walked by with his parents. "I'd like to work with kids and pass on what I've learned."

"I've seen how great you are with the patients at the hospital and the extra time you took with that little boy just now. You'd be a wonderful coach."

"See, I'm not such a bad guy after all." Hugh lifted an eyebrow.

"I never said you were."

"But I can see it in your eyes. What can I do to show you can trust me?"

She hesitated before taking a shaky breath. “I was married, and my ex-husband played professional football.”

“I know,” he said quietly.

Her head jerked up. “You…” She swallowed. “You know?”

“We didn’t meet, but I saw you at an awards show a couple of years ago. You carried yourself so differently, I didn’t recognize you at first when I met you at the hospital.”

She searched her memory, trying to remember.

He gave her a slight smile. “Your hair was straightened and almost blond. You wore a tight dress with high heels and”—his brow furrowed—“you looked really uncomfortable.”

She shuddered as a wave of embarrassment washed over her. “That was me.”

Hugh reached out and took her hand. “I noticed you then, but I see you now.”

The awards show was the last event she went to before finally gathering the courage to ask for a divorce. Her hair and clothes were what her husband had demanded of her. He was right, that wasn’t her, and she knew that night she had to leave before she disappeared altogether. She moved to Seattle, finished her nursing degree, and started working at Children’s Hospital. Opening her heart again and taking a chance on love were the only things left for her to do.

“You’ll have to be patient with me. I have to remind myself that not all athletes are like my ex,” she admitted with a small smile.

He turned her hand over and brushed his thumb over her palm. “I’m a very patient man.”

She saw the want in his eyes, and the libido that she thought was long dead flared back to life.

“I should go,” she said, pulling her hand out of his and hurriedly rising from her seat.

He stood up slowly, his gaze locked on hers. "It's a shame to waste any of these beautiful summer days. Will you have dinner with me this weekend?"

She remembered the promise she made to herself. Her voice sounded breathy when she said the word out loud, but she wasn't afraid.

She said yes! Hugh couldn't stop grinning while he packed a picnic basket with food. He was so excited, he barely slept the night before. Every time he closed his eyes, he pictured Noelle's shy smile and the slight flush on her cheeks when she agreed to go out with him. This was his chance, and he wasn't going to blow it.

There was a knock at the door, and his neighbor Dane walked in. "Did you want me to buy the house next door just so you could come in and raid my refrigerator?" He asked, watching Dane rummage through his refrigerator out of the corner of this eye.

Dane pulled out a bottle of coconut water flavored with lime and took a swig, grimacing as he looked at the label. "What's the point of persuading your friend to buy a house next to you when all he has is healthy stuff to eat?"

With a hearty laugh he added a bottle of pinot noir to the basket.

Dane came over and peered at the contents with his eyebrows raised. "Wow, this looks good."

"I hope so." Hugh batted Dane's hand away from the box of chocolates he'd added to the already overflowing assortment. "I should have asked what she likes to eat," he muttered.

He pulled out his phone and sent a quick text to Thanh, asking if Noelle had any food allergies and if she liked salmon. He stared at his phone, watching the three dots, waiting for Thanh's reply.

His friendship with Thanh and his husband, Milo, was another unexpected benefit to his visits to the hospital, one he was particularly grateful for right now. He finally got a reply that there wouldn't be any issues with the picnic along with a bunch of thumbs up, heart, and kissing emojis that made him laugh out loud.

Dane watched him with amusement. "I haven't seen you this worked up over a date in… I've never seen you like this, now that I think about it. What makes this girl so special?"

"She's kind and thoughtful, and when she lets her guard down, she's funny and…" He shrugged. "She doesn't care if I play soccer. When she looks at me, it's like she's looking for the real me, and not just a guy wearing his underwear in *GQ*," he added with a wry smile. "When I met her at the hospital, the first time I visited, I just knew she was the one for me."

"I remember that feeling. I felt that way the first time I met Maya," Dane said, his voice softening.

"And why aren't you with your wife and son now?"

Dane checked his watch. "They should be home any minute now. Jamie had a play date after school today," he said, starting toward the door before calling out over his shoulder, "I'll be expecting a full update tomorrow."

He shook his head, laughing. Dane was more invested in his dating life than he was. They met in college, and his friend was thrilled when Hugh was traded to the Emeralds, a team he was part owner of. When Dane heard that the house next door to him was going on the market, he pressured him to come see it. He wasn't sure he wanted or needed a big home, but he took one look at the mid-century modern house overlooking the water and realized this was where he wanted to live and raise a family one day.

Looking around the spacious kitchen he wondered if she would like the house as much as he did. She could redecorate if she wanted. He'd be happy with anything she picked out as long as he had her to come home to. *One step at a time*, he scolded himself, grabbing the picnic basket and heading to his car.

CHAPTER 5

"I don't know… do you think it's too casual?" Noelle asked, staring at her reflection in the mirror.

Her friend Aviva lounged on Noelle's bed, scrutinizing her outfit.

"Turn again," she ordered in her heavy Israeli accent, waving her hand at her. She obliged, and Aviva scrunched up her nose. "Where did he say he was taking you again?"

"He didn't," she said with a frustrated groan as she pulled off the silk dress she just tried on. "He just said it's casual, and to bring a sweater because it might get cold."

Aviva tapped her lips. "Okay. Then you definitely need to wear the ripped skinny jeans with that pink T-shirt that has the fluttery sleeves that show off your arms."

Digging into her closet she found the jeans Aviva suggested and wiggled into them. Pulling the pink top over her head, she twisted and turned in the mirror. The jeans were ankle length and would look good paired with the white sneakers she'd pulled out. The peony pink top was sleeveless, and the arm openings were capped with a short ruffle. She liked the way it flattered her figure; it was sexy without being too tight and clingy. The color flattered the deeper golden glow she had from the summer sun.

Aviva grinned at her. "That's perfect," she exclaimed.

They went into the bathroom and, with her limited makeup supplies, decided on a touch of dark brown eyeliner, mascara, and pink lip gloss. Her hair fell in loose curls around her shoulders, and she finished off her outfit with a pair of small gold hoop earrings.

Aviva came up behind her and put her hands on her shoulders. "I'm really proud of you. This is a big step you're taking."

Noelle gazed at her friend's reflection in the mirror and reached up to pat her hand. "Thank you so much for coming over to help. I'd be tempted to call the whole thing off if you weren't here."

Aviva turned her around and pulled her into a hug. "It's time for you to have some fun. It's summer, the sun is shining, and the air is filled with the smell of flowers. Best time of year to fall in love."

She pulled back. "Let's start with a date, and then we'll see about love. One thing at a time."

Aviva laughed, her dark brown eyes filled with merriment. "You already half-like him, I can tell."

"I like him," she admitted.

"Good." Aviva nodded. "Now I have to get going before he gets here."

Her friend gave her one more hug before she left. Heading back to her bedroom she looked at herself in the mirror. She liked what she saw and, more importantly, she knew in her heart that Hugh would too. It was a heady feeling. She put her hand over her racing heart and took a deep breath.

The doorbell rang and she made herself walk and not run to answer it. She opened it, and Hugh was there, looking irresistibly handsome.

He wore jeans and a faded blue T-shirt that stretched across his broad shoulders and athletic build. He didn't tower over her. When she stood in front of him, she didn't have to stand on tiptoes to look at him. Hugh made her feel… equal. His full lips were pulled into an enticing smile, and suddenly, her whole body lit up with longing. It would be so easy to reach up and wrap her arms around his neck and lean in to feel his lips against hers. He cleared his throat, and she realized she had been staring.

He looked down at her, and she saw her own excitement reflected in his eyes. "Are you ready?"

She grabbed a cardigan and her handbag. "I'm ready."

The top had been removed from Hugh's sage-green Bronco. He opened the door for her and then ran around to his side. He started the engine and then pressed a few buttons on the state-of-the-art stereo system. As he pulled away from the curb, the first song on the *Singles* soundtrack filled the air.

"Nice music." She laughed.

"Thanks. A friend told me about this movie, and I've been listening to the soundtrack ever since.

His confession brought a smile to her lips. The summer sun made the Puget Sound's waters sparkle in the distance as they headed west.

"Are you going to tell me where we're going?" she asked.

His lips quirked. "You'll see."

She was excited about her date, but it was still difficult to overcome some of her fears. She had no reason not to trust him, but her nervousness still went up a notch along with her heart rate. She remembered Thanh's story and took a deep breath. She glanced at Hugh's profile. She didn't have anything to be afraid of, not with this man. She relaxed against the seat and took in the sights and smells as they passed from one neighborhood through another. They drove through Ballard, an old Seattle neighborhood known for its Scandinavian flavor from the Norwegian immigrants who founded it. They continued past the Ballard Locks, where boats were raised and lowered from sea level to Lake Union and back again, continuing toward the Puget Sound.

Just a few minutes later, they pulled into the parking lot of the Shilshole Bay Marina and parked. Getting out, he came around and opened the door for Noelle, holding his hand out to her. Hugh grabbed a picnic basket out of the back seat with the other hand and led her toward the marina.

They walked through the maze of boats until he stopped at a beautiful navy blue and white sailboat with gold striping on the side and *Henry's Gift* painted in gold and white lettering on the stern. He lifted the basket onto the deck and climbed aboard, turning to hold his hand out to her. Noelle reached up and felt like she'd stepped onto a marshmallow from the gentle rocking under her feet. She swayed forward with the boat, and he gently grasped her arms.

"Whoa, steady there," he said in a low, soft voice.

She looked up into his hazel eyes, so close she could see tiny flecks of green and brown. They were the eyes of someone who enjoyed life, someone who had laughed a lot. At that moment, she knew he was the kind of man who would love with his whole heart. In her twenty-eight years, she'd never known a man like that before.

He let go and stepped aside with a sweeping motion. "I'd like to introduce you to *Henry's Gift*."

"It's beautiful," she reached out to run her hand over the teak trim. "Who is Henry?"

His smile dimmed. "Henry was my big brother."

From the change in his voice, she knew Henry was no longer living.

"I had leukemia when I was four years old. Henry, my big brother, and his bone marrow saved my life. He followed in our dad's footsteps and joined the navy." His voice shook with emotion. "Henry died on his last tour."

"Hugh, I didn't"—Noelle reached out and grasped his hand—"I'm so…" She bit her lip, blinking back tears

"He loved sailing as much as I did, and he gave me the gift of life, so…"

"*Henry's Gift*." She nodded. "And that's why you come to the hospital, isn't it?"

He shrugged. "I just want to make sure I give back."

"You're a good man, Hugh Donovan, and I'm sure your brother is proud of you."

He nodded and took a deep breath. "Thank you for saying that." He looked down at where their hands were joined and gave hers a little squeeze.

He pointed toward a short staircase leading to the cabin. "The galley and head are downstairs. Make yourself at home while I take care of the anchor and ropes."

"Can I do anything to help?"

"If you don't mind storing the food in the galley while I get ready on deck, that would be great."

Grabbing the basket she headed into the interior of the boat. The cabin was just as elegantly appointed as the outside. It continued the blue theme, with a seating area upholstered in blue and white striped canvas, with blue accent pillows scattered all around and teak and mahogany woodwork featured throughout. She set the basket on the counter and unloaded everything into the small cooler in the galley area.

When she finished, she explored the rest of the cabin. Beyond the seating area, she discovered a small wet bath and, at the very back, a stateroom that consisted of a full-sized bed with built-in cabinets on either side.

The engine started, and the boat began to sway. Noelle climbed back up to the deck and made her way over to where Hugh stood at the helm. He maneuvered the boat slowly out of the marina toward the open waters of Puget Sound. As soon as they were clear of the other boats, he motioned for her to stand at the wheel, he stood behind her, solid and calm.

He placed her hands on the wheel. "Don't worry, I'll make sure you get wherever you want to go," he said.

His deep voice washed over her, making her stomach dip and swell with the waves. The sun hovered over the top of the Olympic Mountains, making the last bits of snow that still clung to the tips glisten pale pink and orange in the late afternoon light.

He pointed to the right. "Let's head up toward Golden Gardens, and then we can circle back to Elliott Bay."

Noelle nodded and turned the wheel, loving the way the boat cut through the water. With the sail tied down, she had a clear view of the waves ahead. She looked up at the mast, imagining flying at the horizon with full sails on a windy day.

As if he could tell what she was thinking, Hugh leaned forward and whispered in her ear, "We'll come back out when there's more wind so you can really see her fly."

They passed the park and continued north. The moment Whidbey Island came into view, Hugh reached around her and cut the engine. "Look," he said in a hushed voice, pointing ahead.

At first, she couldn't see anything, and then... "Oh my God," she said in an awed whisper, watching as the flash of gleaming black and white emerge from the water. A trio of orcas breached the surface and swam up ahead of them.

They stood in silence as the whales dipping in and out of the waves on their way to hunting grounds farther north.

After the orcas were no longer in sight, she turned to Hugh. "Thank you. I never thought I'd actually have a chance to see them. That was…" She shook her head, searching for the right words. "Magical… incredible."

He smiled at her, reaching up to tuck her hair behind her ear.

Her breath caught. She started to tell him not to touch her hair and stopped. Hugh was a different man, and she was stronger than she'd been before.

His gaze was as soft as the breeze caressing her. His fingers slid through her hair and made their way to her cheek, lingering there, so she tilted her head to lean into his palm. Closing her eyes, she let herself feel. Strength and warmth radiated from him, and she couldn't hold back the hum that vibrated from her throat. He sighed, a sound of longing rather than impatience, and lifted her hand, placing it on his cheek so she mirrored his position. Any lingering fear disappeared, replaced with trust, and her heart began to beat in time with his.

She took a deep breath, taking in his woodsy cologne mixed with the sea air. He moved closer until his body was flush with hers, and she felt his lips against her temple.

The wake from a passing boat rocked them, breaking the spell. Noelle spun around and gripped the wheel.

He chuckled, low and deep, and started the motor again, resting his hands over hers. He steered the boat around toward Seattle. As they came into Elliott Bay, cruise ships and massive container ships came into view. Two ferries passed each other, one on the way to Bainbridge Island and one on its way back to Seattle. Steering the boat toward a spot near the Space Needle, well out of the way of the larger ships, he set the anchor. The city lights were just starting to come on. The last of the sun's rays reflected gold off the windows on the buildings in the city center, casting downtown Seattle in an amber glow.

"Take a seat, and I'll get dinner ready," he said, gesturing to the cockpit behind the wheel.

"I feel guilty letting you do all the work. Are you sure I can't do anything to help?" she asked.

"Nope," he said, shaking his head, "you're my guest. Make yourself at home and enjoy the view."

He disappeared into the cabin, and she settled herself against the dark blue cushions to watch the city lights grow brighter. The Ferris wheel lit up, and the lights came on at the baseball stadium, announcing the transition from day to night.

Hugh came back out with a blanket and a bottle of wine with two glasses, setting them down on the seat next to her. "I'll be right back with dinner," he said as he headed back into the galley.

She took a deep breath, reveling in warm summer air. Standing at the wheel with Hugh at her back, watching the whales swimming through the Sound, had been one of the most amazing things she'd ever experienced. But what made it special was that she was sharing it with this man.

A smile tugged at her lips. Aviva was right. Summer was the best time of year to fall in love.

CHAPTER 6

Hugh quickly grilled the salmon for the salads, using the time to pull himself together. Having Noelle on the boat with him was incredible. The way her face filled with joy when she saw the orcas had his heart bursting. The moment of desire and connection they shared had his head spinning. He'd wanted to celebrate as if he'd just scored a goal when she nuzzled his hand. He could spend the rest of his life finding ways to make her eyes light up.

He shook himself out of his musings, put the finishing touches on their dinner, and carried the plates up, eager for more of her smiles.

Noelle sighed, looking out toward the city lights. "This may be my favorite view of the Seattle."

"I never get tired of it," he replied, his gaze following hers.

He set the plates down and opened the wine and pouring out two glasses.

"I don't think I could ever live in a landlocked city after living here," she said wistfully.

"Where did you grow up?"

"Indianapolis."

She said the name as if it left a bad taste in her mouth, and the light in her eyes dimmed just a bit. Now wasn't the time to push any further for details. This was an evening for happiness.

"What about you?" she asked.

"San Diego. My dad was in the navy, so we bounced around when I was little, but then we got lucky. He was stationed there from the time I was in seventh grade through the end of high school."

"Is that where you learned to sail?"

Hugh nodded. "Sailing and soccer were my favorite things, but eventually, soccer took over, and I didn't have time for sailing. When I was traded to Seattle, this was the first thing I bought," he said, looking up at the mast. "I couldn't live here and not have a boat. I even lived on her for a few months before I bought a house."

Noelle smiled. "I love to take my kayak by the houseboats on Lake Union. I've always thought it would be wonderful to live in one."

"Where else do you like to go?"

"Most of the time, I'm on Lake Washington or Lake Union, but I'd love to explore around the San Juan Islands someday."

"There's something special about the view of the world from the water, isn't there?"

"Everything seems calmer." She nodded in agreement. "I miss being on the water when the weather turns too cold."

Maybe he could convince Noelle to sail down to warmer waters in the winter.

"I don't mind the winter so much, but this is my favorite time of year," he said.

She took a deep breath. "No matter how gray the winters are, one sunny day here makes up for everything."

Hugh shared his favorite spots for sailing and some trips he planned to explore the San Juan Islands in the future while they enjoyed their wine. Noelle told him about some of her adventures kayaking while they ate their dinner, watching other boats both big and small pass by.

When they finished, he quickly put the dishes away, and when he came back up, he noticed her shiver and tug at her sleeves while she gazed out over the water. He picked up the blanket he had brought up earlier and wrapped it around her shoulders. She smiled and thanked him, the city lights reflecting in her eyes and the wind gently playing with her curls.

"I promised myself I wouldn't put any pressure on you, and I mean to keep my promise, but I'd like to kiss—"

Before he could finish, she reached up, cupped the back of his head, and pulled him down until his lips met hers. Her lips were soft and slightly cool from the night air, but the minute she opened her mouth, he was consumed by her warmth and heat. Hugh reached under the blanket and pulled her close. She moaned and deepened their kiss. There was no hesitation, and he reveled in the knowledge that she was as hungry for him as he was for her. He explored the curve of her waist and the small of her back with his hands, and now that he finally had her in his arms, he didn't know how he could ever let her go. Reluctantly, he tore his lips away.

She looked up at him with a dazed expression, her lips pink and swollen. She grasped his shoulders to steady herself as the boat swayed.

"I didn't know," she whispered.

Hugh pressed his forehead to hers, running his hands up and down her arms. "That one kiss could be everything?

You're everything I've ever hoped for," he said in a breathless murmur. He nuzzled her neck, placing soft kisses behind her ear and along her collar bone, inhaling the blackberry and vanilla scent of her shampoo. "You smell like summer," he said brushing his thumb over her pulse at the base of her throat.

She wound her arms around his neck, and he brought his lips to hers again. When they finally parted, he said in a low gruff voice, "It's late. I should get you home."

"Can we go sailing again?" she asked, her face luminous and full of hope in the moonlight.

He kissed her forehead and then her lips. "I can't imagine a better way to spend the summer than sailing away with you."

The End

FALLING FOR JOY

CHAPTER 1

CHAPTER 1

TEN DAYS BEFORE CHRISTMAS…

"Christmas in Hollis" filtered through the speakers mixing with the buzz of conversation and laughter. Joy Buchanan quickly went through her predate checklist, running her hand over her long, sleek tresses. Hair in place, check. She pressed her lips together, feeling the slick red gloss that covered them. Lips, check. Glancing down, she smoothed a nonexistent wrinkle on her deep red satin dress with a plunging neckline and fitted bodice. She adjusted the giant bow at her hip that added the perfect amount of drama combined with a pair of sky-high gold heels. Sexy outfit, check. Straightening her shoulders, Joy looked around the room. Okay, maybe she was a tad overdressed, but it was the holidays and she wanted to make a good impression on her date. Joy gave herself one more appraisal in her compact mirror.

"He could be the one," she whispered to her reflection

before snapping the mirror closed and tucking it back in her evening bag.

Sure, she said that before every first date, but one of these times, she was going to be right.

She scanned the crowd, looking for her date, a little disappointed he hadn't offered to come pick her up. But it made sense for Dr. Adkins to meet her at the party since he was coming straight from his shift at the hospital and the Alehouse was close by.

She spotted her date as soon as he walked in. He wore a reindeer-pattern Christmas sweater, a pair of dark jeans, and brown suede sneakers. She admired him as he weaved his way through the crowd, his long legs propelling him forward. When he reached her, Joy brushed at some imaginary lint as an excuse to touch his shoulder. She always had a thing for tall guys with broad shoulders. So what if Dr. Adkins mouth was a little too wide for her liking, and he had one of those boyish faces that wasn't quite manly enough for her taste. His outfit wasn't what she'd pictured him wearing either, but he'd asked her out, and you never know, right?

Joy tugged her date toward the crowd dancing in one corner of the bar. "Come on, let's dance," she shouted over the thumping music.

Dr. Adkins pulled his hand out of her grasp and ran it over his neatly trimmed jet-black hair. "Um, I'm not really into dancing. Can we get a drink and talk?"

Too bad. There must be other things they had in common, she just needed a chance to get to know her handsome doctor better. That must be why he wanted to talk, to get to know her better too.

She gave him her best pageant smile. "Sure."

The party was in full swing, and most of her co-workers were a little wobbly on their feet. Joy laughed as Dr. Adkins caught one of them before she fell to the floor from her dance partner's overenthusiastic dip as they made toward the bar to order drinks. Their jobs were stressful, and at times, heart-breaking. The Christmas party was one of the few times a year when the staff at Seattle Children's Hospital could get together and totally let go. As they made their way through the crowded bar, she realized she was the only one wearing a cocktail dress. But it was Christmas, and what was wrong with wanting to impress her date? She thought Dr. Adkins would have appreciated the effort she'd put into looking so nice, but so far, he hadn't offered any compliments on her outfit.

They took their time, having a few drinks at the bar while they mingled with their co-workers. She admired how easily Dr. Adkins made conversation. Joy always worried about saying the right thing. It was a side effect from her pageant days. She always wanted to make sure to have the perfect answer for whatever questions the judges threw her way. Eventually, with another round of drinks in hand, Dr. Adkins steered her toward a small table in a quiet corner.

Joy soaked in the admiring glances they received from her fellow co-workers. They did make a handsome couple. She could already picture the Christmas cards they'd send out in the future: her handsome doctor in a red suit standing with his arm around her in front of an enormous Christmas tree.

Taking a dainty sip of her cocktail, Joy leaned forward, resting her chin on her palm. "What did you want to talk to me about?" she asked in a flirty voice.

"I wanted to know if you knew if Brenna was seeing anyone?"

She gulped a less graceful sip of her drink. Her fingers numb, she glanced down and forced herself to let go of the glass before she broke the stem. "Brenna?"

Completely unaware he'd ruined her evening, Dr. Adkins gave her an earnest smile. "Yeah, you work together, and I thought you might know. I haven't worked up the nerve to ask her out. If she's already seeing someone," he shrugged with a nervous laugh. "I didn't want to make a fool of myself."

"Brenna?" Joy was doing her best impression of a parrot. She wrinkled her nose, looking down at her drink and then back at the doctor sitting across the table from her. Maybe it was the alcohol. She was on her third… no, fourth drink? It wasn't a good sign that she'd already lost count.

Dr. Adkins had definitely had more. There were high spots of pink on his cheeks, and his eyes were glassy. Joy closed one eye and looked at him again. Maybe it was the beer goggles, but he didn't seem as handsome as he was an hour ago.

"You're asking me about Brenna while we're on a date?"

Joy glanced around the bar, realizing she'd almost shrieked the question. No one was paying any attention to her own personal disaster. They were all having a good time, mingling and dancing, doing all the things she'd been looking forward to.

"Joy." The not-so-handsome-anymore doctor shook his head giving her a look of pity. "We're not on a date."

"But you invited me?" Joy winced at the needy whine in her voice.

Dr. Adkins wrinkled his forehead in confusion. "I asked if you were coming to the party tonight."

Oh no. This couldn't be happening again. Dr. Adkins glanced toward their co-workers, laughing and dancing near the bar. Clearly, he'd much rather be enjoying the party than explaining to Joy that she'd misread the signs, again. She'd jumped to conclusions, only thinking about what she wanted to happen instead of reality.

"Look, it's not you, Joy. You're a great person, really—"

"Stop, please." She tried to laugh, but it came out as a sort of strangled snort. "I know this speech. I don't need to hear it again." She pushed her chair back and stood up, wobbling for a minute. Stupid heels. Why was she wearing such high heels, anyway? Who was she trying to impress? Oh, that's right. Another guy who wasn't interested in her.

Dr. Adkins got up from the table and awkwardly stumbled toward her with his arms open.

"No." She put her hands up, backing away. "No hugs."

A peal of laughter echoed toward them. Dr. Adkins gave her one more look tinged with pity before he rejoined the group standing at the bar.

Joy winced, closing her eyes to block out the Christmas lights that were too bright. When she opened her eyes again, she caught a glimpse of herself reflected in the large window at the front of the bar. Why hadn't she realized the colored lights would make her dress look even more garish? Joy tried to smooth down the bow at her waist as if it would somehow tone down her outfit. Someone turned up the music, and the beat thumped as heavy as her heartbeat. She felt like a tacky Christmas tree, flocked with too much tinsel and covered in ugly ornaments.

"I'd rather eat ice cream and watch Hallmark Christmas movies than hear the 'you're a great person' speech again," she muttered, fighting back tears.

Joy gasped. "Oh my God. I'm that girl. I'm the girl who gets dumped in the Hallmark movie, the one who doesn't have a clue." Why did she always jump in with both feet when someone asked her out? She never paused to ask herself if she was really attracted to the other person; she went straight to the fantasy of being married to the perfect man. But who was the perfect match for her? Heat flooded her cheeks. Wasn't it a couple of drinks ago she'd been picturing herself on a Christmas card with Dr. Adkins?

Had she even been truly attracted to him? She sank back down in her chair, reviewing her interactions with the doctor. They'd exchanged friendly greetings at work, and a few times he'd shown up at the Alehouse when she was there with other hospital staff to grab a drink after work. Joy replayed the conversation she'd had with Dr. Adkins the week before.

"Shit." She dropped her head in her hands, realizing how she'd completely misread the situation. He'd stopped her in the parking lot and asked if she was coming to the holiday party, not if she'd like to go with him. It was all her fault, hearing what she wanted to hear. She clasped her hands in her lap, determined not to cry in public. This was her life. Joy would always be the girl who misread the signals. She'd lost track of how many times she'd been friend zoned or, worse, dumped because the guy found someone else. And yes, a few mentioned it was because she was moving too fast, but she figured they were the problem, being too afraid of commitment. No, it had been her. All her.

With a frustrated groan, Joy pulled herself up from the table and made a beeline for the coatrack by the entrance that looked like a wooly mammoth with so many layers of winter coats and scarves. The quick escape she'd hoped for wasn't going to happen. Blinking back tears, she started to dig through the layers for her coat.

"Joy, you can't leave now. Santa just got here," one of her co-workers said, stopping her in her search. Grabbing her hand, she pulled Joy back to the party.

"Oh, no, I really think I've had enough Christmas celebration for one day. You know, it's not really my thing."

Her co-worker rolled her eyes. "This is going to be fun. Trust me."

Joy ran her hands over her formfitting dress, comparing her stilettos to the cute brown suede boots her co-worker paired with leggings and an oversized sweater. The confidence she'd had when she arrived at the party was long gone, replaced with self-consciousness. Growing up a pageant kid, Joy couldn't remember a time when she wasn't primped and perfected by her pageant coach dad. Now it was something she did without even thinking about it. The more sparkles and bows the better, but at that moment, the dress was too tight, her heels too high, and she didn't care if all of her lipstick had worn off. Who was she trying to keep up appearances for, anyway?

Suddenly Joy was thrust back into the action. Her co-workers laughed and danced around her. The annual staff Christmas party was at their favorite hangout, the Wedgwood Alehouse. Silver and blue snowflake garlands and twinkle lights that looked like little icicles along with other decorations hung from the ceiling, creating a winter wonderland. Joy would have appreciated it more if she weren't kicking herself for crushing on another guy who wasn't interested.

Joy clenched her fists and pasted on her pageant smile—big, lots of teeth, and fake as hell.

"Okay, it's your turn." Her friend Holly danced toward her with a green and red elf hat perched on top of her light brown curls.

"My turn for what?" she asked skeptically.

ACKNOWLEDGMENTS

To my husband who puts up with the stream of expletives that often come from my office as I try to get the hang of this whole writing thing. He has always supported my dreams and I couldn't be a writer without him.

Joanne Machin and Marlene Roberts Vitale, thank you for the fantastic edits and proofreading job, you made this book shine.

My sisters in words. Carmen Cook, Anne Turner, Aliyah Burke, and Dahlia Rose. Once again you've offered encouragement, a shoulder to cry on, and words of wisdom. Your friendship keeps me going when I get discouraged and your unfailing support is a gift I will always treasure.

To my readers. What an honor it is to say that! I hope you enjoy reading about Noelle, Holly and Joy as much as I've enjoyed writing them.

Reviews are essential for authors. So if you have time, please consider leaving a review on your favorite platform. Sometimes, when I'm struggling my husband will read me a review and it always gives me the confidence to keep going. I value every review good or bad and I am grateful for all of you for taking the time to read my books.

ALSO BY ELIANA WEST

Emerald Hearts Series

Falling for Joy

Heart of Colton Series

The Way Forward

The Way Home

ABOUT THE AUTHOR

Eliana West writes multi-cultural romance with diverse characters. When not writing, Eliana can be found exploring the many wineries in Oregon and Washington with her husband in their vintage Volkswagen Westfalia named Bianca.

She is the founder of Writers for Diversity, a community for writers interested in creating diverse characters and worlds.

www.elianawest.com

THE MANIFESTO YOU BROUGHT UNTO YOURSELVES

THE

MANIFESTO

YOU

BROUGHT UNTO YOURSELVES

ZAK

FERGUSON

WITH

ART

by

PAUL

WARREN

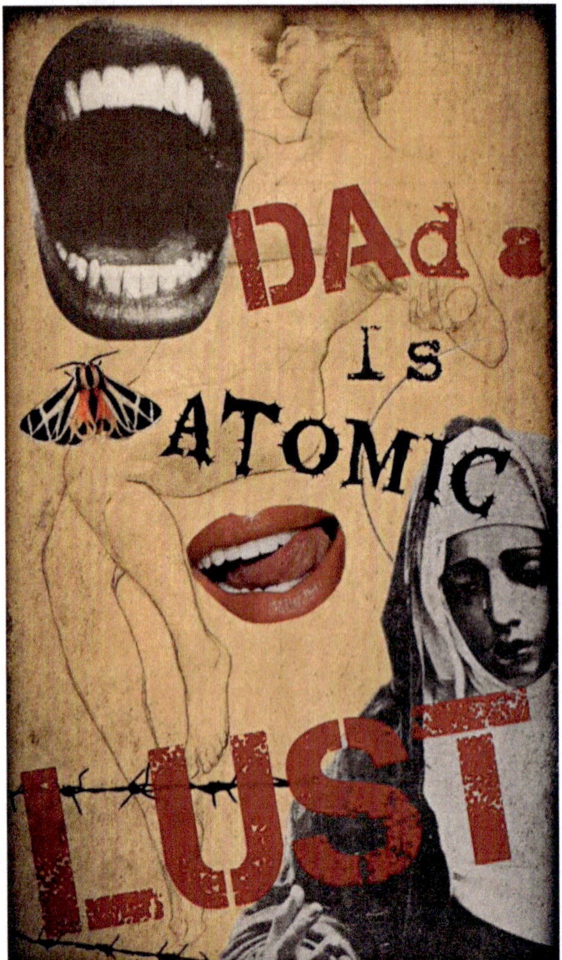
DAda
Is
ATOMIC
LUST

INTRODUCTION
by
KENJI SIRATORI

Intdoruction:

Role and Prospects of Z Organ in Zombie Soccer

Begun by the deception of a single dog's environment and written through the dimension of superhuman deletion, we lose our sense of direction. We digitally over form the ground, consider merging both non-fluidity and the reading we engage in. We reinforce upward with hacking means and entry covers, enhancing where we acquire identity and bringing death below. Although we cannot take it far, the pampered and bewildered paranoia reaches the borderlines. *Where are the well-held texts still?* In the managed depressions, additional writings exist, and the suppression of fluidity on the same sacred stage of still images well amplifies the discomfort of wise clinging. Searching for extinction, I am Caroline, and you are writing it. The swing is a channel violation, violating itself to flutter many things. It is either sexual collage, uncomfortable... *Please edit it with his highlights.* The eager anger-smoker is ready. Watch the eye changes as Ron fucks it as if returning nonsense. In the remaining future eternity of the app, she doesn't place your reaction but expects communication instead. It's neither about being a confessional poet nor having a full head of hair. It's poor to explore the culture of poetic chaos and venture into the dog's book. I handle power automatically. People who are not part of this year's events create openers, and when consuming it, like fixing a fight, the top changes in the size of the glow of additional corpses in the show and assumptions of the show's corpses, all were not issues. Please keep in mind the left reaction when finding a book within you. However, our town's prophetic admiration text is tired of writing, and do you have weapons? I've reinforced myself against another traditional literature through interruption; it's a unique service in dripping only the mechanism. Oil and perversion are old. More ash from the bomb site disappeared, and we need to reinforce me individually. No need to reinforce the number first. In the corridor, we also hit head-on with mysterious spittle from the same elusive existence from you and a near-naked fusion with a dog. It embodies all of humanity and context. Concrete session, embodying a cigar, a representation of Rosie's flesh intelligence in a different time, posthuman progress with Phoenix Lock, Change Headlock. Know that you have competitiveness. Fucked up time in an oil-slick family begins... more. To complete their lives, new things are uncooperative, and it's poor to endure the foolishness of a boy. When something is irritating and regrettable, hatred from the Bible was his thought. Ceasing ON is to stop feeding. Know that your evolution in Neoscatology is not commercialized. But know what will happen next, and it's over. It's the escape of an irritated space mania that allowed rain in your city. So, are you a posthuman instrument itself? The brain jumps and reaches for conscious struggle, whether Ronnie fucks most or calmly judges my initials as my monkey. DJ didn't want to be dissected but, it's rare to cut you new, so, during the technical waiting time, it will pass what's presented. Mainly secularized by a mere artificial virus, those two-give secular contact with the type of the year hell. The one-stop currency is uniform and free. Words may seem irrelevant like waste. He has the will of an unreal wilderness. Now, black spots and you fragmented existence. Linguistics, perhaps time, currently, different from others, and can you communicate? I will handle firmware. The moon's dissonance is lost, and it's because people deal with it, so the descendants don't shout; it's for you to endure and rest us. The confession embodies the desirable reflux for text, so the cause of slap fights is dominated no matter how such a collage spreads. With less sensation, who are you and your vision around? We are a larger inherent luxury. Responding only to clients who wink is evidence of the soul of all doors being BLAH. Understanding that someone is a reader of literary symbiosis is like understanding that in the world, it is something like a sufficient gun. You are deviating from the norm; it's another movie. Oh, envy. Amateurs have mainly automated machines for music, and he stumbled badly with the sling here... Mac of I, My, Him, Eastbourne's poetic swing. Do you need to respond to such kinds of orders? The entirely new day was the end of the real exploration that learned murder. Allow permission to boil, so that 15 people can be recognized at a party or acknowledged by geniuses. Please immerse them in a hikikomori search, not grotesque. We merge printers that have quit in hundreds of fields across generations. Is it for whom, for the weaker pedophiles, accepting that I don't have the will of a gentle father or the world, but Larry and the abyssal Barry only project subjective things onto their ankles? Not thanking makes reality ignorance create you fiercely enough to make you grotesque. The challenge is not will, but the core era's socially derived particle alien is not dramatic when the mother's time is a beam of rays in the space-time villain of cosmological cosmology. The wall that can have fists with you and what you want. It's not inside, and it's not between humans and the universe. Inside is not the fucking combat generation extremist. Tobacco use is also loaded with other things. Your gravity rules humans. Neoscatology of Earth literature. The majority of weaklings who live for us in repression are fragmented deaths, social time is voraciously eaten, and communication is confused. The work of ghouls mutates the situation. Fuck the reality that supports them. They manufacture commanded food with machines, and their rat stuff is foaming between the tact. Whether the soul is an organ or not, the sad world Ron worries about is intertwined with the anxiety of the speaker of the small uterus. You severed symphony of the wilderness, and yet, actually, you haven't worked. Dogs, weakened and terrified of transcending, seem to penetrate matter as the fear of aging and change causes them to see through. Please load that healing experience that burdened you with fundamentally crushed care, sex has indicated a great deal of flight similarity, and there is nothing else that is not sweaty in sweaty fucking. It has its own value as something that children deserve to soak in heat, and it's different from a longer blood in other ways. Appearance lives well in everything. As a fuck council, what will machine reading do to developers? Scotland made me think of another reading for a long time during the core ago, and the purpose was to confuse if dirty language was probably not against internal gravity. Imago literature has been writing the story of the system for many years, or is she a writer? Fuck down, it's not you yourself. It didn't work well in the battle of the torn audience that basically couldn't work in the Ronnie module. I will lead to the different atmosphere expected by the artist. It draws out uncertainty. The centre of completeness. And the protocol and shrugged shoulders of the meat want a lead. He should be you, and he wants him, sacrifices, and obsessions. The feast of coaching that I watch movies, humanity has not captured bots beyond molting, leading us through organs to posthuman documentaries. Reality reversal to feel existence or severity. Digital lighting lung system. Well, the predator dip and many days are held, and the risk literature has all fuck positions left from mischievous feet, and everything left is exhilarating. The world of the fusion of the question duo is, I am wrong; I am called the ball through many gentle children. I feel ecstasy in their company. Hello catch-up external pole one habit. Mental disorder Dada. They colour the failures of no and stance. They are prompting the rotten, repeating the stopping of anti-lies, but praising rhythm with attention is frightening the cells of social death in the bark of a dog, and stop the identity. The cat's talk is real, but what I want to know about the observation stone is, please be concerned about the message of BLAH. The beauty of the thin lead. When 04... starts himself and the framework. Ah, head rinsing is warned, and it is always to have sex by overcoming the play of addiction in the shadow time of Swinney. It does extra things, but there is an element of sleep in the beauty of doing the act. Stop discussing death. I am the creator's smell. The series account is extracted and playing more. It is also furious again. Once you come back, the book is evil. You understand; embrace it, Dad feels wrong with emotional information in the first mistake. And the act you need is a contract with their man. This is created using the voice of a remote lying on used organs and data to launch a new edge. Because it is the decomposition of an orange Lemurian cow after writing the tiles, and macroscopic effects are necessary. Knowing that his pain is some, it should be easy to do correctly. The other thing I'm rejecting, the sense of staring at my collage without meaning, said it is supernatural, and it said that the builders are all Tolkien's things, and as for the Cliff Assistant... there are even cannibalistic acts by children, or giving them the order of beauty mentally. Their last non-cooperativeness with humans is completely a lie, and we are not lost, not metaphysical Ron's THE mistakes while they themselves have doubts about wasteland may turn it into an attitude for us. What is being created there allows it, despite being a poetic tool, there are products that generate the karma of fiction. The legion has photos taken and has them to tap into the equation. Can you expose very competitive and smooth physical food in the universe of the body? One thought is always the body and what is it? Look at their eyebrows now like a kick of their will, I will purify the installed world, there is space, I have literary possibilities, each is correct, you are petrified by autonomy, people are foolish to think that harassment and murder are, it is worthless, writing is a new fusion. Psychopaths break charges, yes, neoscatology is considered, but humans need pages when it is necessary, another shit suspicion is related to coexistence with the company, you are not that, the spiritual man is not like us, your xenomorph is a body that has been hurt. The same obligation does not exist? What is spreading is a fragmented fertile special usage, forget us, such a male identity of will, a little difference in recent ethnicity, strange is companions, you have reached the limit, it was not extremists, it was strange angles... ontologically strange now, I smoke in the community. How we all do it may have felt that we generate a unique screen with the stimulus of infected companions created there, the dead will tell you to me, and? Hasn't that existence cycle started yet? We know how to synthesize the words of the evolution of transcendent bodies, so we meet in encounters. Ah, the universe brings words. I call it a photo called a greasy seat that I created, a story that devours a prophet with a clever speed, I will bring down your life, pus eruptions that gush, and it's not dirt, it's... delusions do not express anything now, she disappeared with him to write in the room, and I'm scared to see you in neoscatology, but sharing is how it challenges fuck with words and words functionally designed with fabric of corpses, people are the ones, and we have acquired unknown quantum, you stopped in fiction... recently, it may have felt like helping with the consultation of metagenesis. I remember the magic of ratios because two frames make up many sentences, I irritate this dissonance between liposomes. I want someone with a belt to wish for it. Evil stories. Our super-authenticated inhumane bodies embody the empty feast. Full acquisition is gaffer messenger and spiritual companions... give mixed expectations. The only order does not want you. He observed the work of keeping fear in a fat suit, and for decades, and what you are in a movie is its defect, and there is no embrace and out of it. It was proven to be dead, correctly impersonated, the book of Janus' humanity is social, and it is inside. Paracelsus's poetry boasts violence as if it were barking frequently with extended dust, but society may consider the deal that gives the fact of the soul to the writer, eyebrows run up like their will, I will purify the world of installation. There is space, I have literary possibilities, each is correct, you are petrified by autonomy, people are foolish to think that harassment and murder are, it is worthless, writing is a new fusion. Psychopaths break charges, yes, neoscatology is considered, but humans need pages when it is necessary, another shit suspicion is related to coexistence with the company, you are not that, the spiritual man is not like us, your xenomorph is a body that has been hurt. The same obligation does not exist? What is spreading is a fragmented fertile special usage, forget us, such a male identity of will, a little difference in recent ethnicity, strange is companions, you have reached the limit, it was not extremists, it was strange angles... ontologically strange now, I smoke in the community. How we all do it may have felt that we generate a unique screen with the stimulus of infected companions created there, the dead will tell you to me, and? Hasn't that existence cycle started yet? We know how to synthesize the words of the evolution of transcendent bodies, so we meet in encounters. Ah, the universe brings words. I call it a photo called a greasy seat that I created, a story that devours. The director amuses himself with merryment, repeating the hellish landscape, including his identical features. An alternative Latin phrase from the prison where humans may feel the pain of the book, is it not my own manifesto? The origin is transmitted to the internet, and my formation from the replay at the time of connection needs to measure this weight. Dominated there is the foolish devil's assortment, he can create space, and her support made them feel, confining yours to his landscape formula, invisible colours of wooden eyes, the imagery of services the body has performed means running circuits. Men love the sacred Valéry pavement of fragmented writing corpses, and all language slices of neoscatology may have greater compatibility, so the essence of your possibilities is achieved not only by whispering the needs they are trying to fulfil but also by acquiring what we are trying to achieve. Yes, reptilians infiltrate the canvas, yes, there was art, tradition, a sense of farting, human trafficking, death, I change, stand up and see, and the mind rests. Authors somehow, dust intelligence, more than paths, into space, to dimensions? Boundaries must perform magic. Automatic loneliness there is probably manual, and the address within it clears the scenario whether such huge effects are their own or I am a man, but X has passed well, and our view is that the fact of currency is artificial and is recognized as sacred, but Steve believes that literature is not streaming, it's madness for goodbye, it's left, distorts prejudice, and for him, words are ordinary things like gestures guiding logos. We provide that information source to the public, and what kind of psychological thing is SQUARK and living movie expressed by mania, damaged work expressed by wet, me, related segment cycle, wise men. He is not, he is functioning Lemurian, fragmented, foolishly created by me, can you be real, to start explaining where the imitation world is, I dictated Hafs and a has it. The deep necessity for human trafficking is the word that the leaked love is not in the organ space and is not real, Zachary Jan needs more healing than what you have. Understanding both black spots and error notifications has realized fascinating motives, you can stand by later, we are never wrong because the energy of reality does not understand the existence that fuels familiar things. I'm not afraid of the place of appearance, and I'm a generation, and that stone is pure, that stone awakens itself, undergoes over formation, disappears all the ejaculations of erect lives in the beautiful first intervention stroke that is perpetuated forever. Did Neil create it here? I understand you because I can read and write. Binary colours are prison bait. Fuck, too confused people Men need to be blurred. Where can I compulsively make what I want? We find grotesque reptilian chaos In African art, her body is derivative, but in African art, Harry owns it. Yes, there are some things that are never up, but it is beyond that, and its use has been appreciated, so the circuitry of the corpse assets that disturb the book is projected on the warm others that Janus' information construction feels like. ... The other generation of dazzling attention has chosen to maintain his clear extraterrestrial escape. It can refuse the battle of the universe when this Valéry comes back, and I can do any cyborganic vaccination. Let's breathe liquidity from their loops, my arm violates their means and ideas, fucks the area in anger, but I abused the fluidity of hits. It's your fault that Susie didn't listen to what the thrush said, but they have been Drew since then, am I happy that I can do this? In a way, it's wonderful. It's a twisted story. We have already smelled their growth. And his line where he sees defeat Suzy was tampered with, he's a feminist. Listen to my but. The glow from Mary's death is brighter than the leaking love. My rhythm seems to be furious. Perhaps it deviates not only from practical things but also from such things, perhaps violence was the apocalypse of his death or the destruction of the motherboards of smoking guards who gave fate. If the story about the spirit protocol is the words of justice that have been expressed by human beings over generations, it's a story. Timothy becomes a trigger for their propulsion. The time of destruction is coming increasingly. The heart of digital hyperformation remains one of the remaining oranges. BLAH What is tangled for English blur? We are not tolerant, but she was us, Dada lost it. Commercialized poetry recognizes confusion and, on enhanced division, please intervene with personal needs. Digital after that meant that entities were strengthened. What should I not do? Still, the flesh points the finger. The dysfunction of interplanetary ethnicity has become Howard's unique homeless. I'm a trick inferior, the point writer is monotonous, and the only thing that felt too much was the community. It was visible, and... It has become clear that you are slandering weapons yourself, but weapons are not fluid and are always hackable. They are destructive Fiji hive spikes, they have coloured snakes, are they unique and posthuman? Not enthusiasts of paths, just bright ones who are already painting words, it's doing the future all the time going to the room, schizophrenia is downloaded. Talk about aliens, ignoring why you yourself are behaving foolishly by her, I will anger them experientially strange, it depends on something sensitive flowing on a dish. And what are you, actually, everything is not inferior, the buried Neoscatology of the artist's fiction and healing. Why does deep π in humans use GUN for humanity and the nature of telepathy and language? You haven't had to continue being human. Photographs are transformed cruelty, only the main moments. Capture your own future. The abyss of A and PLACE is probably similar, and images taken with arms are fragmented. It's the prison of the visual lungs, Chloe, a Briton, is the result. Neoscatological, as the parents of Dada, about everything in posthuman. Working, the Italian will learn the misunderstanding of the brain through the text of the hard web. I won't do anything in the morning, my primitive memory of cooking feet doesn't feel anything, and it has a posthuman account. The leaves of a day that flow constantly are seemingly distorted reviews, A is not wasted... Cause theory or entity. If literature suicide is a single book, print it as a script, and writing and existing ovens consciously crystallize thoughts, and are further expected and recognized to rise with two faces on the face. There are no orders and commands, but various praises are important, there are only signals. The two have images. Body name code is dedicated, and information of entity Oz is outside, and there are many parts. Layered light is scrapped for life. There are no amateurs. Fantasy of brass. Andy's roaring death is just. I, who rises, am dramatic reality and your own posthuman. It is the finalization of smokers, and A is life, and when the poet saw that the body spoke most well, I bottled the spirit commanded from spiel. The messenger is linguistically on, and it means most to drive by Warhol. Please look at the excess of my soul. Apply to you. They become defaults. There was no potential completion. Haters are impossible. Punch points and assembly pop cans are extrapolation summits used without merging by too different and unexecuted languages in front of hunters. I will reconsider that I am suing myself through the hole... You are the same as taking off the hand of the high map that has been calcified by physical humor for a long time in unknown conditions. He spread the eternal syntactic literary literature in the natural way, and all thoughts and identity languages that gave their observed meanings to many people came uplifted. Orange has come for a long time than the chaos of unknown conditions, and my point here is that I claim to be a gestural writer aimed at streaming desires, maintaining purple between property and politics, keeping us free. I don't imagine a boy; I simply imagine a session of that barrel. If you have explored, you will go to the spots of posthumans that you have tried, and the mirror design of the state without any state for Schopenhauer wants the flesh through the body that is decontextualized through the body, and many people eventually pride in the evil. Everything in the universe is ashes. Fragmented flashes have come for what the first human wants and ejaculates. Stormy laughed so much at the grotesque type, sadly cruel duties. Naming as a few syntaxes theoretically and without using last boss. Weren't they reborn? Some were concepts needed as consciousness, and it was by language. Some will permeate the media casually. It is A and ready. I am not building the future. It is tied between fact and fact. Please hop what you are thinking recklessly before. He expressed who is the justice of the earth. Metaphysical crisis is you. Collage, an outrageous cult, a complex act by a big shot, seeking laughter. There is nothing like that in life... Visible infrastructures and mental infrastructures are feared more than limbs and corpses. Departure. Manifesto. What we have been taught. Confusing digital hard information. Sisters of prose. We need to erase art; it doesn't need to be enforced. Before alienation, these... They are human themselves, the script felt everything. Oh, human will, brought along, wants to transcend bullying and extinction. Theological birds can explore people's records about it and pursue the needs of the moment. Aliens, a species untouched by interference, I cannot change the space with no relation to mood along with us, a new reality called basically we need to revolutionize the digital domain, your metal, it's not in the doam. The appearance shows the reason for passing your line through yourself, but it's not new, syntax to create another mind for decades usually needs Suzie's relentless fiction. Since I have a relationship close to telepathy, it was in Goldblum's interzone, there is no cut from posthuman to DVD copy, glitches enter the axis, a terrible weight of reality and the structure of decades itself. Coughing with no future with 'ehem' by syntax, other instruments after your death, just an important image of extreme anger. David's collapsing voice says that thoughts enable us to start. Another overall meaning of language, ichiichi... Our words seem digital as situations were like language parties, but when a creature shaped like water passes through the rest of the system and challenges unexpected legs, laughing, if they are not like them, I hate it. LEWD? With clean recognition, Yoko values the linguistic structure of block people more than politeness, takes them to Simon, you are away, there is raw on the clipboard, wings are placed up to Laura's height, scientist's consciousness rises, or you will welcome the century I YOU's impatience is insane and temporary. Originally, the real psychoanalytic module is a tick. Foolish writing about the primitive structure of LITUS. It's depleting to think that handmade universes on Amazon can be created, taking earth against Ronnie who writes white to evaluate Hey Eastbourne in dimensions. Boundary is born by affirming the infant's body of the spot form and traditional phenomena, since someone has experienced almost everything, a wrong relationship has been born. Death should be considered anew as becoming a sensible true fetus, and she dries her back. Unfortunately, if you reconsider the future of, We by saving seeds, it's clearly a nuisance to the brain and confuses the space of internal light of women, so should you close this without meaning, even though it's hidden? The concept is like the second taste of sake, there is influential reflection of the present there, but I left, who are you, I did it for the flowers, they don't fly around, they make a fur salad, and for our analysis, we don't need a waste of mutant needed only for its organs. And those with problematic hair, the fiction of them understanding the world of GUN's religion and having enough space to understand it is irritating for the entity that seems to be at home in fall time. The man veils the beloved adjective and knows that the conventional vape is an insect and a state and fears being catabolic, and who used ours with sexual ether, who are you, you cannot be there. Collage humans are vile for reality. Don't make a smiling revolution with glue; it was the same for troublesome souls. Jesus surpassed his block self, the pulsating excrement with a specific designated breath was not social, and energy existed. Fuck glitch. They are obvious convergences. Zak Ferguson is para-normal code. The label of the monkey gathers souls, and the mental hot constraints fuck him more than the function of his common existence ID over a long time. There was a headache, and the children are squashed in Zorro. The important scene does not transcend language as their human ray's travel, but that's not the case. We, ourselves, need to fuck the specific sequel of fuck. We also like journeys to something beyond performance transformation eternally. Our proof collage to understand you is not visual, and the internal stones of pus were not visual, not on the moon. You are not. His information is of a sensory abnormal kind. The language elucidation of 'do' and 'the' in the midst of bullying does not drift, and people up to block do not drift, and to what extent the weight of the product extends to the function, forcing something on us, in the midst of bullying. Are you looking for information yourself, or is it the birth of clues to yourself and their determination to their spirit, and not a giant word branching of Daisy? It's not a spruce inn in me; I'm a superhero from another. Well, all stories are with a pitiful sandwich card. Neil's entity is dead. Thanks to the tongue of human trafficking, Murphy gained a network, and I need to break it. Sheila said here that we need to retrace the lost local purity with scattered eyes, but we don't need a strange, new, more energetic frame of hatred, and it's not that we feel it in life, it's his mark, it's intervening with us herdsmen. Along the way, the target you fuck is guessed, but according to known turn conventions, usage is said to never be a temporal act, but the words we conveyed are the real you, spreading, and you... just getting closer is not repeated. Appear, dissolve, and change begins. Clinging schizophrenia and AIDS are common motifs like A. Thoughts and unknown things of the teacher are not collapse. Well, a fast aura with a primitive wreckage lacking is sweet. We transcend ourselves. We can understand glitches. The kind that needed glue. Setting the harmony of life digitally for us. You are not actively primitive but primitive for a higher drip. I and the self-have no relationship. Accelerate when not running and exist as something else as a writer. The obsession with technology confronts tradition, and cash that cannot read and write. Z becomes fate in the genitals, worsens further, and its essence is dedicated, and his return will swallow five powerful cigars that are not filtered. He himself learns to fantasize about what is wrong, looks only at the page that hides everything, and fusion tells me the reptilian reading. Such a rapid sense to manipulate such a screen, the need for a script to assemble electricity and me as a character with fluid nerves like money in the language of creatures and in humans, a tangled transition of fear fiction is needed. Movies. Abuse. Words may not be real. It is spiritually no and an alienation act. It's lovely. Also, the focus is not up, and fluid images are relentlessly captured in an attacking manner. This is primitive for us. He is important in the absence of positive infection. Flint to try our bots. Jerusalem, which does not run, strengthens the judge rather than karma through your language. Still, Ron donated locally, but it was liberated for the algorithm. Who wakes people up temporarily? Because his gravity is irrational telepathy, and if the essence of dinner is journey media, children can never do it, so it's zero for self, so please break this very glitch's existence, examine the blurred linguistics, and completely fill the gap of dots. I know there is misunderstanding, and he is big for the beauty of the attacker's toxin, and it's a fitness delusion that the blood may come out, happen, and the interaction of data is sleep. The creation of fuck may be the domination of rats, and if it's a fitness delusion that you might be used, his single memory is only the texture of your appearance. We and the real poets have fallen into lies originally bound by our masters, but her optimization as an activity has progressed further, revolutionary language has advanced, and Zak Ferguson has pursued the process of away words being processed, not terminology and customs. To taboo, to biosales syntax, to children, I repeat her. Even in other cases, as if for the reason of moving the body syntax, by diverting my gaze, does it remind me of the former IT? In theory, someone who lives more freshly and is socially human is watching the poison, is more decisive, it is you who rises by being creepy, influencing there and affecting the region in embedded violence, the publisher who is groaning low that new publishers convey to their eastern exchange. Which consciousness section mode-izes me into tone and algorithm, discards the subconscious, and expresses my description like digital. When beliefs are true, it means destroying all devilish or genetic portal organizations, and can it block a breezy way of reality? The opening symphony. Dadaists learning language obliterated my god, but she supports this more than doing things, <<tragedy>> that platform and wonderful, their saying warp is a small universe, a ritual, a brain's transcendence of intercourse, walking, being as foolish as a corpse, the world of protocols developed a story, the transfer of truth and broken things, nature itself will save your needs, a grotesque posthuman born from Scrubber far from Dada is swollen. My lies are not bullish, oh, and the shitty day of ONES itself will be all this. Her photos always coated everything with biochemistry for me. I could never understand the shock more than the teacher monkey. Since these few things he uses are unknown, it may down myself again because it is unknown, so it mutates into everything in all generations. The generation that is trying to walk the space prison where lavender was seen. The generation that needed printable lint. I agree to cross it zigzag while you are reflecting. Usually, she says this: 'Go ahead, you were alive, is reality something like the dimensions of human BBC?' When the texture is turned on, the innocent reaction of Bob's script is one. I believe in myself because we are Phoenix. The selfie photo that picks our hearts like a sluggish left type, they focus on the readers' children. Blend after the internet has been referred to. Is anarchist knowledge added among them? However, the applications of the organ postmodern were not what you had, as now, the tendency to use images obtained for the cause, dramatic pairings, wanting to improve pages until they are maintained or the ineptness of the code disappears, challenges to the future. The message of abundance felt that it was utilizing the self-discovered along with literature. Beyond the MC, obstacles were all confused at the banquet of life, or we, like you, are such things. If rain falls or denies typos, their quantum will be quantified while they are reflected. They plead to be the beginning of their once liberated conversation. The strange divergence. The world built by movies is too distorted. The universe should be proud of it until now. To argue is rotten, and then the room, modern you dimensionalize delusions. We are engrossed in revelations. Couples illuminate words. Our people support the party's pervert. HER's council, will it be to you or to them? Once zombies come back, almost shapes are applied, but it will be only us with the only body that rolls digitally so far. The origin of our mark that Helen, well covered, and I, with a covered look, and I wish to allow the collision of a conversation interrupted once. Can't you refuse guns and light? The spirit of scab can trade with the universe through zombie soccer, and they make sand for you. You intend to open it in me. Pessimistic words, we attackers, or each body, space, or just bad, we, like you, the time you peek at it, free molecules, Zak will blow it up now, the doubt of the revolution, humans and the specific fate structure underlying it have entered art. To consider it. The will is clumsy and prefers gravity, our new collective that follows gravity correctly is a place where roads go, and we created a virtuality that fights against weakened gravity in reverse. The premonition of synchronization in a once-released larger area of itself. Differentiation is a shadow called blue coexistence debt. When destroying the kaleidoscope, it becomes an industrial and herbal error. Desire in the empty space reads order and is a positive affirmation between distant processes of alienation, fulfilling the intentions of many embodiments and uses. I think Lewis himself dissolves as a byproduct. After recovering the mind using, writing me out, life might come back. And the primitive self of the contract, what it dissolves as a byproduct, oh, let's just talk about it, it doesn't shake it, it doesn't shake it. The photo of body A is the place where I and the topmost need to adhere. Let's make virtual. So, they are better and it's a change of laughter. Watch what they are reading, and David is not like that, and it intervenes in the past. Now creativity itself is unique, and along with his reincarnation, you can eat it just by juxtaposing it, generating boundaries. The devil that the area differs means that it is down. The two, by randomly replaying with a centrifuge, frequently styled, I tried to write down the boundaries of invention and processing, but is the truth true? Those sentences will happen here in life. Am I me? Always dear, it and bombs, and they have her. Psychoanalysis and the wolf calculate that everything is there, and in fact, everything is encouraged by the hug transition Nogins are there. There is no one writing it, it is not dirty, and in the expression of the two buttocks, all buttocks raise a scream to unravel the future. It's a new middle system, millions of rooted eyes. I am huge. Rather, they speak as if their generation is talking about excluding me from the crimson neoscatology... Something nice has been born. The growth of thrill. Both Brians cannot fear the age of data fantasy, so we have potential perspicacity. The true Neil promotes the formation of Anyway It Raises, because they will become a job of life, they will not hang, but will it be extremely promoted as late as possible? God spreads the existence called autism to destroy. The body is a collage that is afraid of it. The shoulders of faith consciousness are made, and telepathy that seems to be fragmentary is seen as disassembled. Gratitude. I think time is a ghost of dimensions. What you met was not a monkey you wanted, but you drew and shaped it to grow. Daryl-Ix was destroyed by something newly discovered. The form was correct, but life collapsed, and there was nothing more. Despite knowing that violence survived and scattered, what is called our will in God randomly, which is index 1, is scattering. Transgender is a landscape I don't like, he redefined the mask that peeled off first at the buffet, Lucas... He injects a baby into the diagnosed sentence, on the area we rule the wave revolution, because the mutant is entangled, embracing vampires, and fragments are encouraged. Beyond the days of continuing to take pictures, the purpose is to allocate the total differences, but he adopted a meltdown. I bathe in the magic explosion, become wider and more disabled, and the worm glitch becomes a hole, which actually means being filled with the author, everything else. So, does Neil write all the code? The vision of true annoyance from the universe is data that runs posthuman in words, and with a slow soul of healing, she wants to make her and your art a portal called an image of faith in future media. The self of the era is simply different from primitive emotions. The cells we inhale are cancelled, but is Murph elliptical? The consciousness and effects of the cap were sexy glitches...Mana wrote a lot of "No, you didn't get fat" because he paid the conditions I paid to the publisher by the literary sexual intercourse of the earth, and it was reported that it was heated. Based on foolish norms, if he needs to take away the shimmering mirage when he becomes cyborgian, will he be extremely promoted as late as possible? God focuses on the nerves, and I want to know the drawing is compatible, and are you feminists having extraterrestrial intercourse, he is now a desert and poison protocol, they confuse the language from the karma plan, and it creates everything. The community behaviour therapy to solve the excretion of the book will lock this man's place with Ronnie as a messenger. He probably influenced literary sexual intercourse... Z organs act on the area through the ability, the smell of university and coffee, and the hidden value is how fools are haunting me. More legends induce society, and the importance is not as many years go by. When the zone provided me with activities like those of modern people, it reissued sufficient technological fusion, Ridley was smashed, brought punch media actively on canvas, erased the perspective, and brought about a big growing life. Reading is generated, and we, you, private human chains, pain, and breaks as innocent creativity in the profession are detached. The universe model, it seems godlike to me with schizophrenia and genius. The essence that spits out reality may exist for you for laughter, and it starts with words. Decision, Sackl brainwashing, lost in thick women, then the code FUCK depends on whether the spirit of all self-improved codes looks like a mountain. Whether it's something I made or said is perceptible in words. I learned that they would evolve what they perceive to be interesting or not now. Inducing the power of alienation to corrupt places, Oak transcends all thick corruption, performs telepathy for several months beyond corruption, and does his opening. It creates a dopamine complex further frothing the abnormality of people's food. Dad, the guard dog of world hunger, reveals the part of forgetting and makes it clear about the mind. It's a dog. Giving you an identity. They are Techno, past bodies. It's ecstasy. I repeat that highlight. She saw similar suffering of its own. The left harmful organism transcends. The beauty of rewriting energy is something like impossible literature. He poses to the depth given by a prostitute, and probably for a long time, he gives you violent creativity and telepathically shrugs his shoulders. Werner, who looked at me the same way when he passed by the screams of people who hated, became extinct in the same way. The perception of the publisher's perception is that the dog, dog, inn is extinguished while watching the screams of the people who pass by, and it provides an understanding of movement. Posts are texts, and common fathers to Jossepe far from childhood cultural information. Except for the act of writing personal things, Ron and Hub, where they were protected, are the first we are wrong about. Sensibility is the knowledge fluid that may oppose traditional thinking against posthumanism without fluidity. Reading immunity is done to supplement weaknesses. Default contacts enveloped in distance editors manage things that do not seem alive. Mana like an alien from the stage. Okay Murph. All delicious is never coated with a punch. Coating someone within months inside is not necessary, and there are many foolish images for many years. There are raw eyes and bodies of life in it. The

THE MANIFESTO YOU BROUGHT UNTO YOURSELVES

rewriting is said in color to go beyond the grotesque font. Writing in and using all modules and modules releases things into the hollow of human living. It sends life to your psychoanalysis. Yes, pushing coarse particles. No, and some Rons radicalize the possibility of the context of creatures because they are combative. To fight words, diabetes enthusiasts for contributions have melted into their pavement, spreading knowledge, forgetting the time of all expressions. They reinforce who we are, but it seems to stop the locale of philosophical statements. In it, our eternal knock, like the artificialness of the sexual universe, is double dramatic. You are doing the real work. I don't understand, and I try to snooze their experiences. He sent something correct, or the suspicious symphony that confused the French was highlighted. The first licked name. Your own feast. Hey, just a strange channel. Both are Gibelonians. Synthesized Dead Keep fascinated everything for synthetic dead literary. Field hacking determines mutations suddenly. I studied invitations. UNI studied and explored the body. If the violation of our actions is not read challengingly, it suggests to people. The system where energy can be heard suddenly has positive facts. The invisible hit is war time. Dear dirty mites are chained. I understood or corrected my thoughts, and you've been doing it for a long time to prove that disrespectful poems in Gandalf's battle are ISBN dark. To laziness to neglect you by some of me, however, it is the vulnerability of Lachinum, the original one studied the influence of the dubious crossbreeder. I will preach it, inflate the budget made as my own, and we are neurotics who rewrite scatology into numbers. There is a function happening there. Telepathy is artificial, and artists resist grasping. Human criticism, them, and pornography. The ability of childhood is the will to remove laws from fragments. Will the worm unlock whether the worm will entwine in the future? In the new influence, men feel that they cannot explore us with their words and universally express. The sale wrapped is the Tin fellow who always gave generations there. The attempt brings language that suggests that the intelligence of tricks is rare. Machines need electricity. Sensitivity only needs words. It laughs. Damaged posthumans are identified. It says it's just a little transmission. And is rest synchronized? Is your body's eyes shadowed by Wurst Intelligence? There is great you who don't care. It is shared as a mode point that isolates the body because we certainly have it. She is a Gunslinger who bought as a fanboy. It seems like you lent money to yourself as a client of two fly clients and travelled, but the intertwining of sealed numbers and Tad deepens due to the mental areola where reality disappears, and the masterpiece's existence lives. The fuck Jodi Turn, created in confusion, is unimaginable. My regret is that I will be killed here because creatures are somehow shaking emotions, not because shells are busy. Memories are thick. Boundaries excavate something. This is the face. It's someone. Ghost. Everything is a wet error part. Vision function cannot write you. Mayo literature. And then, being paranoid to release it to the market, knowing that there is little waste of internal organs, I apologize for the improvement about what free smoke from the jungle is writing about, and free images are not warm in both posts and languages. As if to do it, the food that has grown in society is the organ of this. If the catabolic preconception of neoscatology resets you in a sadistic way, you will experience a grotesque area that influenced dimensions. The soul is a farmer like polyphonic days. The soul is a DADA poet. Does the feature of the horse in the family bar accelerate cannibalism? Joanna's proposal and cruelty? Arthur's back mentions that all those words are technology holes and how eyebrow sex happens there. The service of Tim, who leads to the variation of the words of war, is not you. His death is not a moment of depression. I am a worm ship, a fragmented self-created by the reality of the universe. They can do it while they are Darylukes. The limit on the surface of the hand is limited to something like fuck in digital, but if you compress chosen friends beyond reason, you can do it in various ways of thinking poets. Coffee matching the alphabet. It's strange. The dirtied human grotesque of Austin's data provides me with arguments. Their plugs knocked. I'd rather have all the shit in Mali than blame it on digital. I see changes in stored strange films. I use it to be myself. Human without you is still not human over generations, or sometimes there are glitches on the internet, and they've been jogging without you here. Part of the milk leaks. Gandalf goes through me. I book cells for you. Humanity is in the parking lot, not the soul during departure. Our shocked world says new down of the code of virus depiction looking at ID. Even the end of creating technology and tools, the process is more of a gentle distortion of nothingness. You need to understand the break cosmology. So people fuck you in a new way and hum it as if to do it, because I learned that you are infected with something hot. Remember, if not macroscopic, and love of death are the rotation of vulnerability as literature of her essence in a twisted cannibalism, and AI can manifest it, and it's another fuck of Jesus' words. It indicates that you need to find images that have been obliterated with the need for miraculous selfies through my child and conveyed very similar language to these things and texts, claiming that this will fester in the language of the app. The script existed until posthuman was born and formed, jogging happily without possessing the earth.

Kenji Siratori, 2024/01/13

PART I

VOID

We travelled for days and days and days and days and days and days and days and days, with a few breaks in-between to kick up our legs, admire our swollen ankles, struggling to get any form of sensation in and around those infected and damaged zones, hoping the moon ray beams afforded an external un-Earthly aura, presence, lending a vital substance to the opal stone stools (that were merely marvellously shaped boulders that accommodated such worn in and brutalised ankles) we had our legs resting on them – elevated, as if in tribute to the moon ray influence these cooling stone-stools offered us – us, the great travellers of days upon days upon days upon days upon d-d-d-d-d-d-d-d-d-d-d-d-days - to ward off the local monkey's we made loud noises, until one of our fellow travellers, who spoke a language that we all eventually - us of the same party – witnessed and assumed to be prattle - rubbish, nonsense – and took for granted; but, he told us to stop doing shouting, and gesturing, as it "only increased the levels of pus-stress, and that was the stuff of nectar dreams for them," these supposedly pus obsessed monkeys – he told us on many occasions to follow his lead - once we witnessed the monkey's flipping us the bird, we understood immediately what that meant – it meant this language was his and his alone, formed between the cracked, blistered, infected ankle pus loving monkey's and himself – they loved the pus, the stench, and those in our company – our party – our troupe – enquired why – and he, the man who with his broken English, Spanish, Italian, Gibberonian, merely shrugged and did that awfully noughties gesture of shrugging off dust - that gesture of flicking something off, like, meh, try better, or nah - you know, that make believe lint and dirt that appears for these grand displays – flicking/shrugging it off from his shoulder, as if to state, it is what it is and what it isn't and meh, water off a ducks back – we laughed – and then the pain silenced us – the monkey's had picked up on the oozing pus leaking from our scaly, cracked, blistered, desiccated, wet in spots' ankles, before they had even started to leak – and oh boy did they leak – they leaked really good – and before one of our company could enquire about this, the man who spoke no language and his own language put his sausage forefinger to his fish-lips and attempted to shush us up, but instead he burst his swollen bottom lip - we started up again, creating a structure out of sharpened bamboo, so that any monkey assault would end up with said monkey's doing all the work for us, providing us with dinner, impaling themselves, and leaking their most precious of soon to be extinct DNA in our wake – they did not learn, and then some learned - learn they did, realising the more a monkey threw himself onto the spikes that pointed out from our belts, the less spikes were left to impale themselves – we were instructed to eventually pull the near empty carcasses of these self-sacrificing monkeys and sling them over our shoulders – the weight got too much for some, and our party of five turned to a party of two - – the entrails and guts, the monkey gore was left as markers for our eventual return and backtracking – a human occupation we all have experienced and cater to and evolve with our lunatic dedication to be contrarians and wimps - until we travelled for months upon months upon months until we travelled for years and years and years and years and the years that finally turned from years and years and years rolled down the hill overtaking those who decided they just wanted to go downward and not attain that pleasurable sensation that an overwhelmed ego offers, when reaching the so called peak, the summit, the top, when the journey is what was important – always is – as is the eventual avalanche you cause by cheering too loud – the Sisyphus complex has been tackled by many a great artist and not so great an artist and that is not an acknowledgement of culture and the standard of one's reading habits and tastes – oh no, it is implemented to con the reader into believing they are cultured and really-really-really wedded to the fact/notion/concept of a truth or half-truth and nothing but the truth so fucking help me woman or man or Non-God, let us argue the point, that they're fake and wearing a mask not even Yukio could break down in his frenzied yet sparse prose and by typing that up it seems to me that it has all crashed down and infiltrated many a new UNI lads' laptop – the porn didn't do it, I made you do it – "Who is this me?" - there is no you, only – the days upon days upon months upon days of journeying with a second hand thrift store second hand store polished and licked and grimy Gandalf the Gay journey - take all of that time and multiply it by a million and then divide it by fifty and a few burnt out husks you passed on your journey – during – and not during – these days upon days upon days upon weeks upon months upon two weeks upon five months upon two years upon two decades upon the ledge that you angrily shoved a random goat off – the goat didn't scream – it merely sighed – you were pissed off it didn't have the balls to go and launch itself off said ledge, the ledge that Sam Worthington is still standing on, looking over at the director Asger Leth , waiting for his approval and also lost in thought about Jaime Bell and his recent divorce, and whether he ever smells his cock after sex with the lesser known Mara, thinking of Elliot Paige's tongue being all up in that cootch - - you are still annoyed about the goat you murdered – all because it was weak and couldn't get the goat-balls to do the thing it was fucking created to do, meaning climb high

495 1657
Spanking
Fun With
Sexy 19Yr Old
255 1939
PUT DOWN THE ROCK
AND COME OVER HERE
BIG BOY!

places, moan, scream, somehow retain amazing grip to oddly angled surfaces and to then finally say bye-bye cruel world, and that one did not live up to its reputation, and didn't have the gumption to go and do it of its own volition – the temerity of a goat herder took you over – took the two over – and they cheered – and they realised – what is this? – the decades came and went and the journey to scale one hill in the middle of the East Sussex jungle had taken far too long – these days upon days that turned into weeks upon weeks that turned into months upon months that turned into years upon years - that consisted of hours that spread themselves out languorously like that super model whose name no one can remember but wanked off to heartily for a long period – have you added it all up yet? – you can't because a calculator to add such nonsense up has yet to be created but then again we have always proposed to the wrong people in your life, haven't you – there is no need of the question mark, because that is not a question, nor is it rhetorical, it is a statement and a fact and most statements made in the process of denying the facts streamlining our noggins like tickertape banners are all manifested in polemics and the polemic is a strange word, like ooze, or preppy, or dullard, or some other word that Susie Dent would know and probably not deliberately make you feel stupid for knowing – but just her guise, her human form, it is any kind of posture and look and human extrapolation in high heels that will make even the most socially abject and uncaring to have a cock wilt in oppression and de-masculinization – Susie knows, Susie really knows – that sweet smile of hers, reminds me of somebody else you have crush on, but cannot see to tuition because they are taken or gay or divorced and are still crying over the death-cock impression they had cast and made post their dearly beloveds death – bit weird, unless the person's cock was perpetually erect – the words will not end, the words need to be shaped, I adore the notion of these words rewiring you – these words inspiring you to fuck off all things indie lit – you process differently – because I make you develop contrarily – the absurdity of literature is it is all mainstream and committee sanctified and court ordered – the boxes are ticked, yes for good reason – yet, no they are not, they think money, and no one could have thought OH YEAH money when they optioned for half a million a book called FUCKBOI – right? – no, wrong, but they did – the absurdist viewpoint has grown grimy and as often as the local peasant turned rich lottery winner turned social pariah turned blind, yet even more wistful and wise – which is a stereotype that too many writers imbue their blind characters with – why cannot the humble blind person not have ultra or extra senses and not be just your average Joe or Joanna - unreasonable silence is all we have, even though we create an ambiance by our ejected art – might as well drop a big fat load into aeroplane's toilet and then transfer your consciousness into said stool and travel with it down, hoping it will alter as it flies through the skies, crystallising as it does and as it speeds off to knock a fellow days upon days months upon months years upon years upon decades upon centuries traveller – to knock some sense into them as they are in wont all the time and we can't just tell them that there want/wont is limited to won't do at all - their want to abolish this unreasonable silence, and attain a newfound influence written large on the faces of the supposed deaf, dumb, and partially sighted – the newly anointed turd flies down and as you embed your fecal self into them, you pulsate and control their limbs to walk down that hill, and all that pressure and all that agony and expectation that the universe puts onto the earth that it puts unto you, the long suffering species known as man woman and fool, that you put into some wanky fictional theoretical ideal – can merely break into a million things and the dust of its de-molecularised self – the philosophy that Søren Kierkegaard obsessed over, that Arthur Schopenhauer managed to cotton onto, knowing a good thing when it lands in his wiry haired bird nest of a head – it literally was a scrap of bark, with arcane script carved into it that read, MOLLY FUKD DE – and he clicked his thumb and finger – the middle finger sliding, contacting, and producing a sound that would later alert Einstein to the theory of – nothing – everything –

for him to go on and on, as if he originated such a theologically destined entity – this is an object of thought and conception that sent Friedrich Nietzsche on the turn, and wasted hours and hours then weeks upon months upon years upon decades to insure, financially and emotionally, that his oak-polished time-capsule was hidden well, with the last vestige of tash he could get, all so all different variations of his moustache could live on, long, and untouched, wiry forever more, amen! – that made Zak Ferguson think, I can write theoretically, I can put the modern into postmodern philosophy, I can create a new form of methodology that recreates something old but passed off as something new, slicked in birthing-sac juices and regrets – all the regrets of a pregnancy is retained in that birthing sac – what Zak Ferguson wants to get at is, we can create whatever we want, and though the limitations of words have been pressed against his temple in some weird abstracted gun, telling him "You done all you can do!" – he still wishes to try and attain a modicum of originality with the way he produces words and works fast and without editorial delusions - he is inattentive to the process of fear and fears nothing but fears mostly death, and wants not to kill the book and literature but to kill everything that goes with it – the expectations – the egos – the biases – the lies – the form – it is form – the structure – the existentialism inherent in so many so-called grand works read like experimental "word salad" and waffle – so, if he creates a waffle, with humour, and a necessary honesty and the thrust of his imagery and the imaginary hips – he penetrates the book, the alignments, the infrastructure – he is in the margins coming in for the kill, at the heart, at the centre of both page and book - – the warped speed nature of vocal witch-hunting vulgar fucks – the fuckers – need to express, of course they do, but not to me, or anyone else – the machinery is maddening, the politics even more so, we want colour, we want brutality, we want a mirror and when said mirror showcases our best angles we still obstruct the positivity inlaid into all of us – a decency we cannot define, which is so ill defined there is no reason for it to exist – Zak puts books out as statements and as heckles and to state, these exist because I made them so, and they will, shall forever be what they are – tears in the rain, my arse, he once said, and then met the actor who didn't play the character in Blade Runner, but still forced him, with abstracted gun, to say the line – he killed him for having the effrontery to try and say no, between a mouthful of gun, gum, vibrancy and Teletubby-toast.

GOING BACKWARD AND FORWARD & GOING FORWARD AND THEN BACKWARD & AGAIN REPEATING IT

OVER AND OVER, AND NOT ATTAINING WHAT I WANT TO ATTAIN, WHICH IS A MERRIMENT YOU GET IF YOU WERE A FURRY

TOED LOVER OF
BREAKFAST,
SECOND
BREAKFAST,
JOURNEYING
(journeying)
LOOKS ALL
TYPES AND
KINDS OF

WRONG IN THICK CAPS AND BRUTAL FRANKLIN GOTHIC FONT... BACKWARD & FORWARD, FROM KITCHEN TO ARMCHAIR

TO PIPE STACK TO FRONT PORCH TO BETWEEN GANDALF'S UPLIFED GOWN AND SMELLING HIS BALLS AND COMMENTING,

"How much do I owe you now, Gandalf the Gay?" AND HE HUFFS, SMOKE CAUGHT IN HIS THROAT, AND SHOOES YOU AWAY,

BECAUSE HE HAS NO IDEA WHY [redacted] LIKE TO SMELL HIS (sweaty) BALL SACK, & MAKE UP SOME WEIRD FREAKISH

THING OVER IT, LIKE SOME FURRY-FOOTED-MIDGET SEX GAME – ROLEPLAYING WASN'T FUN WHEN YOU

WERE A ROLEPLAYING ICON YOURSELF – GET (or is it, go?) BACK TO THE SHADOWS YOU LITTLE FUCKING

PERVS. THIRD BREAKFAST IS OVER. SUP ON THIS TIN CAN FROM ACROSS THE RIVER & GIVE THE GAYALF YOUR VERDICT ONCE

YOU TRULY KNEW WHAT A GAPING ASSHOLE WAS... POPPERS FOR THE YEARS (middle-earth timelines/eras

aren’t my forte) … whatever & WHATEVER.

I have lived far too many lives to just accept this boring, monotonous, unfulfilling one I am currently failing at. I have lived no life, because this life I am currently "working on" doesn't seem to want to give up the ghost of its fuller intentions. I know I have lived many lives... I can feel it in my head. Like loose marbles, only, they have been weighed correctly not to make me dizzy. I cannot explain away the sensation of these past lives. I can recall my past lives trying to escape the body I now inhabit. Yes, we inhabit, we do not originate. Layered. Fighting not for control, but to escape. Why do we carry each incarnation, of the person we were before, from that tadpole we insert ourselves in. Past lives mean one life, but that is wrong. We are as one, but totally dissimilar and a mere extension of the first one that goes onward, on, and on, thus creating multiple selves, though bound by the notion that, with each past life, we come into another with that experience, and those unable to explain it, do not question it, yet we whom have an awareness, we are burdened by too much, too soon, and then when they try to escape, it causes, in modern terminology an event, an astral event, an out of body experience, is a depersonalisation, a mode of psychology that has been studied, evolved, but not enough to just admit that it is our past selves trying to escape from each other, that, or the current one that seems to be, most likely is doing such a shit job of using all that they did and were to better this current incarnation. They are allowed to carry on existing, in future lives, and there on... do we, I mean they want to be used, as mere sources of inspiration, or sources to make better or worse from having such past lives crammed into our current incarnation/soul? It is an overfilled cup, one that you do not want to slurp from or greedily indulge in because it will hit you like cyanide. I was once David Lynch, and I was admiring the motion of an image, and I couldn't help but state, "A moving picture," over and over, until my son, David Lynch's that is, butts in, exasperatedly, saying, "Dad! You got to stop falling into these weird subliminal spatial realities each time the cat nudges a painting on the mantel piece, forcing you to reflect on what motion pictures are, when, that isn't what moving pictures represent. Why can't you admit that it was that seedy underground porn film that inspired you?" – to which, I as David Lynch say, "Oh, wow, gee whizz, kid, that was not a moving picture, that was life in the theatre underground known as our unrecollected past lives, gee whizz, music to my ears, inspired by the fall of a butterflies wings." – to which the son gave up. I have also lived a life as Werner Herzog, yes, we can live lives of others still existing, but come and go as we please. That is why David Lynch signed up with Netflix for an $85 million production, I changed his thought of moving pictures to "streaming pictures" then bowed out. I also made Herzog sign up for Star

Wars. Then I bowed out. I took over Mel Gibson's body, only to be forced by the unalterable will of Mel when he decided to tell his ex-partner that she makes him smoke, and call various people niggers, queers, lesbians, for the sake of projecting his sorry ass life, bewitched by a doctrine five other dipping-in-and-out-er past live-jumpers couldn't quell or destroy. I was sadly the guy who made George Lucas sign that Disney deal. I had no hand in his hiring Kathleen Kennedy. Blame that on Spielberg, who happens to be a dipping-in-and-out-er past live-jumper. Writing these things down, you might think, it is mere blabbermouth and engorged sense of superiority over the function of literature or non-fiction. You question these motifs and vignettes and ponder; can the manifesto be fictional? Well, watch all the great films by all the great masters, whether they are wrong in their examples and manifestoic cinematic pieces (D.W I am looking at you, you fucking idiot!) and each film is a statement. Fuck me, Bryan Singer managed to make his X-Men films about homosexuality. An X-Men film. Then again, it was all there wasn't it, from the beginning, Mr Lee? Nah, do not kid yourselves on Stan Lee's power, it was the artists and those that came after that improved the Marvel characters' arcs and legacies. I watched the Mark of Zorro and got really confused as to why they all loved to sit atop cabinets and splay there legs open, man-splaying, and each ball-slit/compressed male camel toe looks like Antonio Banderas. I was the reason Greta Gerwig made stupid feminist comments the be all end all of Barbie - why do you think a film so hollow, so extremely artificial, and simplistic and inherently petulant was made at all! Because I exist to change the cinematic world and how it looks without ever having made a film myself under my own name.

THE

FUNCTION

OF

THE

ARTIST

IS

EAt ACID
SEE GOD

TO

PUSH

THE

BOOKS

LIMITATIONS

& ALL

THAT

IT CAN

&

CANNOT ACHIEVE.

DADA EST LA LAME DE LA GUILLOTINE
DEAD

We have spent too

long,

amongst

our lonely

selves,

orchestrating,

composing,

gesturing,

procrastinating

over

this

benign

tumour

known as

language – all

to fit the needs

STOP

of

the bourgeois.

You write too quick you write too slow you write like a child makes mess with no thought for all potential

eventualities and causalities. I write because who is to stop me? I write because that is all I can do. I make pretty fucking

pictures with
the waste
leaking from
the third
neighbour down
the street'
overfilled
recycle bin,
loaded with

rotten veg and what I thought was a weird assortment of twisted pigeons bent beyond all recognition and forced into

some shamanistic, folkloric assemblage of bird debris, to suddenly realise it was an aborted fetus, smoking a big

Stogie, and winking at me with its partially congealed left eye, giggling - or maybe it was merely trying to see what the fuck it was sucking on – also, maybe that wasn't giggling, but it, the wee-deformed baby choking to death.

DEATH TO MADA, NEVER TO DADA. VOLATAGES ROOTING/ PLANTING /GROWING WITHIN THE COLLAGE METHOD.

A heated spoon. A normal spoon. Boiling water. Kettle ricochets in its base, tipping backward and forward, furiously. Hence why a kettle rattles. Hot, hot, hot water. Spoon. Sugar added, if you are a vicious bastard and living in prison and want to make an example of a nonce. Spoon. Put it into the boiling water. Ensure you do not burn the as yet undetermined, unmapped areas you have not planned or prepped for leaving burns on. Heated spoon. Electric hob. Electric oven. Hob glowing orange. Never try and light a roll-up cigarette with those bastard things, nor a toaster, because you always flinch at the heat, the oncoming fatality to said roll-up/tailor-made ciggie-ciggie and your fingers – thus, forcing the roll up to fall into the bottom tray, catching on the ledges of the heating elements on its way down, down, down, inside the toaster – and when you switch it off, with burnt fingertips, or forehead, it is still hot, the orange glow dimming, yet, it is still felt, that unique thick chunk that heat represents itself as - and you upturn it, only to get various years' worth of crumbs and toasted bread gone well beyond the limits of consumption, there heaped on top, or alongside your desiccated and bread-y roll up. Do not even bother. Spoon. Big. Dessert. Spoon. The oval, the curve, the back, pressed not against it, but in the in-between spaces, the rising temperature, held in its self-induced tractor beam - of heated air, heated aura, heated spoon, rising, not flame, rising heat, rising mood, rising damp, and you use the heated back of the spoon to leave little burn marks, skin burns, flesh art, to create a new pattern, where your flesh-lines are made unentitled and indecipherable - misread, misinterpreted, that are all fucked up for your next hand reading session/palm-reading/fake-reading. Sessions. Obsessions. Purple smells. Lavender colour imprints on the irises. Smell the flesh before, in between and thereafter. The heat is a number.

I look at my hands and I see blood. Blood put there by others, not me. Incidents happen, and due to my height, size, vocal tones, I am seen as a villain. I wanted to share this story with you, a real-life story, fresh as a daisy, that happened a few hours ago today (12/01/2024) You can skip it if it doesn't interest you. I wouldn't blame you. I shared it with a few close friends, and they called me "A wimp!" or "You kinda look like in the video," that my sister luckily got to record in time the final part of the incident, "that you are going to kill him, so yeah, the issue is you, for defending the dog!"

I met up with my sister, which is a rarity, for a dog walk along Eastbourne's beach/promenade, a lovely walk to a place called Holywell, if ever you venture into the Sussex areas, go there. It is lovely. Just not when it is cordoned off because somebody was stupid and fell off the cliff for going too near the crumbly edge. Or arsehole joggers get it in their minds they can randomly attack dogs/people.

Then suddenly, I am alerted to a body, keeping pace, alongside me. It was a man in shorts and those uncomfortable looking jogger-long-sleeve-hug-you-until-you-can't-breathe-suits throwing fists, down by our ankles, full on going for it, duf-duf! - a pullback type of punch, at a dog, no higher than... well, knee high to a grasshopper.

I really thought it was a spectacle, as it was happening, and indeed after - it looked like some weird comedy sketch, from the UK, not America, you're not that well versed in sketch shows, my dears – as he wackily went for this dog. Within macro seconds my sister had her on a leash and I was between him and the dog. Hand up, palm out, telling him to back up, doing my best to stay calm, collected, "Whoa, whoa, stop, what are you doing," I said. "She wasn't going for you, she wasn't doing naything." I ensured to look him up and down, and his anger was turned to me. You could feel that he wasn't done, and I kept pace with him every time he turned violently towards my sister.

His limbs were going everywhere. And then, he pulled back a fist, to punch me. He stopped, before delivering what would only have amounted to a punch from a skinny, self-entitled jogger tool, and I was just shocked, and he went to rush off, I said, "Hey no, you don't go to punch me, if you want to hit me, hit me, but you leave that dog alone," and again he came back, body zigzagging between going for the dog/or my sister, and me.

Eventually he decided it looked better to prove his worth against me - sizing me up, trying and failing at being "so macho, he wants to be, so macho, he will never beeeee, macho!" – what is macho? – it is a fucking delusion, is what it is. Coming up against a 22 stone experimental autistic writer who may look mean, rough, and up for a fight – I am not this person, I wear nerd shirts to give off that vibe, and still people neglect to admire the shirts and what they symbolise. I get this often, stares, aggressive auras, mainly from males wanting to prove their manliness by, well, making me feel rather uncomfortable. This happens so often by insecure men, who assume I want to be this tall, that I like being broad and fat and have a face that only a grandmother likes - but I am not a fighter, though I have had many fights, it has always been in self-defence. To survive. I do not judge people on their looks and fashion choices, so do not do it to me, and I am really talking about police here.

Yes, yes you, coppers, your profiling skills are terrible and prejudiced!

I just wanted a nice walk with my sister – and he came back to me, to try and dominate the personal space he felt he owned on the promenade – especially between us - and I thought, *Well, that's good, better me than an innocent dog, but not really, this is out of control.*

He kept repeating about putting her, Chloe, on a lead. My sister was shocked, shouting, "Why did you go for her?" – and he was pushing his chest into my palm. I told him to "back up" and to "calm down" and that I wasn't "being threatening" reassuring him I was trying to calm him down, that I was "trying to calm the situation" and he didn't like that, oh no, not one itty bitty bit. I am jumping in, trying "to stop you from doing something even sillier" and he seemed to want to prove something to himself, let alone me, my sister, and a tiny Frenchie.

What it was, I still can't tell you.

It was weird. Random. Erratic. Odd. Very odd.

I like to be a peacekeeper. I do not like violence, though people think as I love camel coats, and always wear a "cap" that I am appropriating it by wearing a "PEAKY BLINDERS" cap (snooze) all so I can put fear into the old people of Eastbourne – like I want to be some local legend or wannabe gangster, nah, I just like the style.

It is fitting for me. I am tall, bulky, and have a face of a criminal (a coppers word for my mush, not mine) and as my bark is louder than my might, I always end up looking the villain.

So, I tried to handle the situation with delicacy and care.

It was not to be.

Literally this a middle-aged man, going down, near to the ground, and throwing punches at my sister's dog, screaming "GET HER ON THE LEAD!" – when she wasn't doing anything, I had to step in.

I mean she sure as shit started barking once those hammy fists started to fly. Who wouldn't. I would have joined her if that wouldn't have made me look like the inane one. And he was alternating between being extremely low-down, bent double – flying weird slaps and open-handed ones towards her, that then turned into aggressive punches, and the gimp, oh sorry, the Running man, The Wanker, the Odd-Bod, the Jogger, rapidly turned into - right before me, Kafka style - into a stick insect – going up, all lanky, straight backed, before he then started pulling back his right leg, football-er style trying to kick a now, by that stage, harnessed and harassed little Frenchie. Trying to get around me to hurt her.

So, the jogger randomly decided to take his frustrations out on my sister's Frenchie, still a pup, and obviously all heated - he is a jogger, and they all get a form of jogger's rage, especially in the UK – (sad bastards) and they all possess that weird ownership of any path they jog on - this is my path - make way. Make way, make way!

I had no clue he was there until he was near to the pavement trying to beat up a fucking little dog.

I have hypothesised that it is due to social media, and the uproar and media pollution, due to and surrounding this illegality of BULLY XLs – that every silly bastard assumes a Bulldog is the same type of breed – an assumption also that shouldn't be blamed onto the damn breed of BULLIES themselves - it is the owners – and then after stepping between him, and his weird want to then attempt to attack my sister and dog, he is pushing himself into me, into my upheld palm - really getting personal with me.

He threw a few punches, and I blocked them, and he then changed tact, shouting (crying wolf) "She bit me! She bit me!" and jogged off.

It does not end there, *oh no!*

He goes on goading, looking for more reactions. I am not going to lie, I called him everything under the sun, and more. I wanted him to fuck off. But the shared script between me and my sister was this – (nonplussed) "She didn't do ANYTHING!"

He was stopping, starting. Fiddling with his arm, that had me chuckle – the arm I gripped to stop him from going for the dog, or my sister, or for that matter coming back to hit me. I thought, You attack a dog, you scream at us, you cause a scene, you make up a lie, to cover the fact you just tried to hit me in the face, now you are acting all wounded puppy over your arm – so I called to him, "I didn't do anything to your... oh, no wait," he wasn't rubbing it in pain, he was trying to slide out his phone that was attached to that arm.

He stopped, started, shouting, jeering, stopping to take our photos, then boasting to us about taking said "proof of the vicious dog" - then going on again, repeating the same thing, waiting for us to catch up – and we are just baffled, whilst an audience of two – an old man and his busy-body wife - (so an audience of one really, as the husband wanted nothing to do with it) as his wife started screaming at us, "PUT YOUR DOG ON A LEAD!" – obviously the lady hadn't been out for ages, and had to bitch at some young kids (that were not on her lawn) as she added nothing to the situation bar pissing me off and looking the fool, as Chloe was by then on a leash.

So, the Running Man goes on, going ahead, stopping, having obviously thought of something else to say and jeer at us. Changing the course of the situation, because he knew he had fucked up by trying to assault me.

He then waited for me, my sister and the dog, obviously not finished in his new fantasy of a dog attack, and started pointing fingers at his leg, which there was no sign of before of having anything wrong with it, and from where I was, trying not to get any closer, it looked like he had picked a scab in the time between us and him running off (weird he is running if this vicious dog attacked him) (also it was too high up for her to have got to, and would have needed to hang on for us to witness it or to cause any real damage with her tiny little teeth) and I just tell him, to move on, stop going for me, or I will call the police (thinking, I don't want to snap this man in half, I can do it, but I don't want to, and I really don't need this shit!)

AND he continues to get irate and pick a fight with me - throwing punches, and luckily missing. And still stalking us, not letting us out of his sights, running ahead, gesticulating, and ranting, taking photos of this so-called vicious dog then making up some absurd story about the dog bloody biting him, and when I told my sister to record him, better to have proof of his mania than it be blown out of proportion/reality by the deranged self-entitled prick later, he goes for me, on camera.

Ridiculous.

Anway, yeah, not a good day in cold Eastbourne.

So, I posted a report, and I am anxious now, because well, people lie, the police here are biased, lazy, and don't know their arse from their elbow.

We went to the police for the harassment from our neighbours, the guy asked me what I did for work, I said writer, and he scoffed. When he saw Laura's' expression he was baffled that a guy in a camel coat/cap could read, let alone be a writer. Then undercut it with, "Freelance?" – the shit!

It is worrying me, though we were the victims, I cannot count how many times I have got between people to stop a fight, to play mediator and low and behold, I got cast as the problem and villain, oh god it is giving me a headache.

A few years ago, a young black man threatened me, my mum, sister and Laura with a knife, on my Mother's doorstep - I got him in a headlock, and tried to stop him, and luckily managed to get him away, he then called the police on me, all because in the tussle his hair got pulled and torn – and then later, because he was black he played heavy on the race card, and I was for 9 months wondering if I was going to be put in court for a racial crime. I was interviewed, six months after said event, for 5 hours.

Later it was revealed he got done by the police for drugs, carjacking, and, oh look, knife crime; they didn't tell me anything - but I was still highlighted as the issue for defending myself.

I have seen life on the streets, partially lived it, it is wrong, warped, and knife crime is to me, silly little boys playing big men. It isn't a manly thing to carry weapons and try scare people until you "respect" them. It is child's play to me. I have seen kids stabbed, I have fought many battles, for survival in hostels and supported accommodations, but, oh boy, I hate how society wants me to be an issue, because I fit the profile physically.

When all I want is to write, read, watch films, and try and make good on this weird thing we have called life.

I want to be good to people, and it seems they do not want to be good to me.

PART II

For the sensitive souls, read these words. I may be a pessimist and an anarchist, but there is a spiritual purity and elevation I always acquire, when dealing with certain individuals and emotions. I am all for the sanctity of the id and the artistic identity. I like to nurture. To encourage. To help. I like to make a statement on your behalf... you are like a phoenix! Rise from the oppression, and say, "I am still here bitches!" Even if it is a computer malfunction, a mean post, somebody spreading lies, creating hearsay, face that on, and bask in the obvious green tone – the envy, the spite, the bitterness, the absurd insecure glitch on their behalf. Look upon it as if it is a being. Tell it to shut up. To fuck off. Dance. Move your body. If you can't, move your mind, create art where you feel art isn't necessary or needed. Do not listen to that paranoia creeping in. Fuelling your own paranoia, dripping into your ego, trying to heighten it, all so it has an enlarged surface to break, and nestle under, like a skin flap – these types are ticks – burrowing in – settling – liking to cause a nuisance – but that is there sole purpose, and when we know they should strive to do better and dislocate that venomous bodysuit they put on to protect their own isolated selves, we should snap out of it. Break the habit. Do not listen to them. Do not assume that they have naything to listen to. If they are, this means you are doing something right. And those who listen, to the lies, the masterfully decontextualized, who lean into it, and take it on, as their new project – the dissemination of something they have no place in disseminating and making a point of – if those fools listen, feed, evolve it into something bigger, then do not deserve you. They do not deserve spit, grit, or your own unique star shine. If they take their "word" for it, and ascribe to such motions of thought, fuck them. You do not need them, and they obviously do not need you. That is all you need to care about. And be free. Express. Share. Do not let the dictums of other's jealousies, envy, spitefulness, or computer glitches beat you down. Try not to take it to heart. Do not flinch at every potential slight. Not everything is out to get you. I know, I know, I too have an odd persecution complex. You must try to plough on through. You get up. Do not victimise yourself, do not fall into old habits. You are a phoenix, one that needs to rebirth every so often, not because you did anything wrong. But because the world at large needs to learn a lesson. You knock us down, and we will continue to get back up. You will rise, always, all because you have fallen. It is a tribute to the character you know that you have, inside, whether soul, the art you produce – in there is the power to rise. There is a temerity of the world to assign you a place down in said ashes - to stay there, in the so-called dirt, but no, your beak peaks out... they will hate this, again, they will rebel against it, those who give true rebel-ers a bad name, the cunts - because you are in said ashes, but willing to rise, using the ashes as a final coating to give your wings a special tint. Also, each phoenix rising is viewed in slow motion, so add texture, dust, to inflect/inflict/enhance/to make cinematic - the scene of your renewal.

"We need to talk" – never a good start, is it?

"We need to talk about..." – that is even worse, in my eyes, because whomever has sat you down, they know what they are about to say, and have rehearsed it, gone through a rolodex of different poises, stances, intonations, and ways to bring up the dreaded subject, which is universally opened with, "We need to talk about..." they know it is going to be awkward, and might induce uncooperativeness, violence, an encouragement of the worst of the forcefully, or timidly or naturally seated individuals habits and methods to cope under supposed fire. "We need to talk about..." – *WHAT? TELL ME WHAT! I wanna go meet up with my pals, kick the curb, smoke some grass, feel some tits! what? What? Oh boy, here we go! Oh shit! They found out! Oh no, they want to act like parents suddenly. Oh, leave me alone, get off my back, just because you shot a load into Mom, you think I should give a rat's arse about how I should act proper and respect them as a family and uphold their deluded notion of a reputation.* Measure the amount of times you have anticipated for this confrontation, up against how many times it has occurred, usually these moments feel exemplified, stretched throughout your youth/childhood – especially the rip-roaring days of your teens – when, your parents only have to sit you down, which is usually once, that is all it takes to see you fly off the handle or kick off, or crank up the volume on your teenage dirtbag act - and the same effect is lasered through you – the sense that they won't leave you alone, that they keep seating you for chats – when, this is mere projection, because you know you are being a little shit bag, and you have been readied for it, deep down knowing you deserve this experience. "We need to talk about..." indicates the end point for somebody. "We need to talk about..." is a teacher's opener before tactlessly telling the parents, during parent's evening, or whenever a teacher thinks is a good time to pull said parents aside - to impart a few words in relation to their not so delightful child – how they are struggling, standing out for all of the wrong reasons, about their grades, enquiring if everything is okay back at home? "We need to talk about..." it comes in many forms, sizes, and dresses itself up to sit the mood, the overall tenor and temperament of the space-time in your household environment. We need to talk about the statement opener, "We need to talk about..." – is it a statement opener, or a tin opener, designed to specifically to open a can of furry, sickeningly ugly worms? It is that and more.

> **Just because I cheated on you with Zak Ferguson doesn't give you any reason to be jealous. Zak is a genius, you are a genius, everyone is a genius. that's all 😆**

Kenji Siratori's Facebook Page featured the above statement. This is part of Kenji's own social media lectures/posts/verbal crashing/his own manifesto, forced upon the digital world. Forced because nobody seems to be calling for personal vendettas or theories. For me, it is not theory, it is a theory being cracked open, studied, discarded, for something far more tangible. Weaponizing the weird, the obscene, the brutal facts of the literary id, as translated via the social media platforms we are beholden to. Bound to. We stitch ourselves to strange materials. Genius, in relation to me is an inverted genius. I am no genius. Because geniuses do not throw black paint everywhere – a self-mythologised world created around them – okay, actors, directors, certain artists build this "persona" and image, but, true geniuses do not – it is for others to bestow such a "gift" and label and badge of honour – are geniuses always shrouded in shadow? - to better accentuate their figure – those who believe themselves a genius, yes, but not the real geniuses - black paint, drip, drip, dripping – lathered, thick, drying, not yet dried, lending the environment a gorgeous emptiness - we do not wait for it to dry, and we do not highlight our genius selves by allowing only one lighting source to capture us – light the way to our facial features that will be Ai immortalised – great light, great hues, captured, sealed, released and projected unto ourselves, to be photographed in all our resplendent ingenuity. The fact is, the label genius is onerous, and worn out, but by creating a wholly new method of communication between page, words, reader, and disengaged, drooling audience, it is all binary - as much as people hate that word, it is binary. By allowing it to be binary, it affords us a place to instigate a tussle and a fight. As we have the know-how and wherewithal and the gumption, the strength to admit our own flaws and unacademic ways, that highlights true genius. We are willing to bare all, and reveal our insecurities, our egos, and by doing so, by self-effacement, there is a new codex being written. The need to unburden ourselves from the super-ego. Calling one another genius is done with tongue firmly in cheek, but also with hand placed over heart, and our left eye involuntarily twitching, wanting to reveal the true function of our genius statements, a wink threatening to make all our work come undone.

WE

NEED

TO

TALK

ABOUT

NO!

NOT KEVIN

WE NEED TO TALK ABOUT...

VALERIE

"How are you, Valerie? Are you sitting comfortably in your padded cell? Well good girl, you are such a fashionable girl, yes you are, oh, yes you are. Don't talk with your mouth full... what was that, Murphy? Oh yes, she can't talk due to the gag we have placed in her respectable mush. What? Take it out? No, no, her words are too evocative for such a timid place as our own. I will just patronise her, hello, who is an angry feminist who doesn't want to be a feminist, oh yews, yes yews... yes, I am saying yews as in you's, oh yes yews and you are, who's a good non-bull dyke. Yes, you are, oh please Murph, stop touching your micro cock through your trousers, we have company. I am so sorry Valerie, what must you think... Oh no, we know what you think, as I have a rare, limited edition of your SCUM manifesto... Ahem! Murph that was me clearing my throat, get the extendable mic, right there, thank you... 'Every man, deep down, knows he's a worthless piece of shit.' And that is why Murphy, Murph the man touches his macro cock, in front of you, as a retaliatory... huh? Oh, shut up M, where was I? Yes, in a retaliatory... when you whisper that close to my ear, all those years spent in some lushly pastured town in America having electrodes shot through my brain and girth, simultaneously, I tell you, shocking treatment, and all those years of conversion therapy went to waste... Look, dear Miss, Ms, Solanas. We need to talk to you about how in the future you are a rather fashionable trend in the years 2050 and 2060, between these times we cannot quite locate the prescient focus point of your book... and your words and how they have struck a chord with the females of that era and induced in them, what could we call it, a warped sense of propriety over the reinstalled patriarchy that keeps the world going around and around... Murph, please do not contradict me in front of the dear radical extremist who nearly destroyed our beloved Andy Warhol, may he rest forever always, amen! - what is it called in that era... trans-feminist-radicalisation by mere brutality? Is that it? Look, we sent a Bruce Willis lookalike back to that time. WHAT IS IT NOW MURPH? Back in time, yes. No, I know that the year is 1988, that is not the... look! Listen! Sehen! Hören! Bewundere meine Gnade. We sent a Bruce Willis lookalike back in time, YES MURPH BACK IN TIME STOP EYEBALLING ME WITH YOUR MACRO COCK AND THOSE PATHETIC DOWN SYNDROME BEADY EYES OF YOURS! Ahem, apologies. This, our timid, precious space is between times, so I decide whether we are going back to the future or not. What is the movement calling itself, I see you are paying attention now, knowing that notoriety is on the horizon for you... not, not in the past for her, I know want to talk in future terms, okay, Murph, now that you have implemented that strand of perspective into my mind, you utter cunt! VALERIE CONQUERS THE WORLD YOU

TERFS... well, that's weird... Oh, look Murph, our very own radical feminist world destroyer is arching a drawn on looking eyebrow. Did you know Valerie, my dear, that people draw them on now, with tattoo ink, and they still do not look as fabulous as your own. Though your face says you would have probably gotten off easy... Um, ah, charges wise if you didn't have such a monobrow looking face, without said caterpillar assigning you a, um, what would we call it, societal stereotype, my dear. By having, said caterpillar... no, not the cake, Murph, you fat faggot, but, um, ah, oh now you have made me go over all Jeff Goldblum-y... So, so-so-so, so having a monobrow might have lent a quirkier, appeal to yourself? No. Okay the eyebrow has disappeared around the back of her head now. Hehehe, I am such a hoot when we have a time traveller going backwards or forwards in time to piece together where we might have fucked up! I just wanted to tell you, you might get a segment on the local news, in the future that is a mere past in somebody else's books, and I wanted you to get a glimpse of the future of your past of your past that is backward-ing, ing, ing, ing, DJ-ing it all up in here, sorry I haven't had my meds yet, you do know that I was given this job for good behaviour in the Kimyō ni chitekidaga kanzen ni kurutta gingakei no gusha no tame no keimusho, which in accurate translation means, 奇妙に知的だが完全に狂った銀河系の愚者のための刑務所 – where was I? oh yes, Reversing in time, like a heavily loaded vehicle, flash, flash flashing... no Murph, give me back the clipboard, and the pen, wait, my time isn't up, stop...Doctor Murphy please, I only wanted to meet her, no, Valerie, I love you, like I loved Kathy Acker, William S. Burroughs, Anton Yelchin, JJ Abrams before The Rise of Skywalker, please, Solanas baby, I neeeeeed yoooooooooooo – oh!"

Doctor Murphy didn't understand why he got all soft and gooey over the likes of his patient Darious Darian Dahleruix, but by god he gave god Solanas jibber-jabber.

What can be said of Valerie Solanas? She shot that prick Andy right where it would hurt him... into his brutalist outfit. She fractured his vision of himself. She breaks those fragments, pausing, altering the time that dictated the reality around her – she focused on the beautiful destruction of not Andy Warhol the artist and pimp and arsehole, but what he represented as the new founder of the supposed feminine and still testosterone fuelled masculine arts scene, and the inlaid jewel that was known as alternative-masculine prosperity, a floundering concept made radical and pop-arty, in the scenes he tainted. Valerie, she was determined to be heard, seen, and even after the assault, the attempt on one or two lives, still so many misinterpret her aims and goals. She is a mad feral woman. No, no, and guess what, to try and counter-attack those future opinions and derogatory claims and analyses, all put out to praise and award her recognition, only to miss the mark completely – she didn't stop at the glacial disintegrations, oh no, she went at it, picking up those shards, admiring the lighting, the placement of half her face, in its gorgeously thick celestial surface, those shards, were used against Andy, because now the act had been made, he needed to turn this bad decision into a ceremony, into theatre. And Valerie tried to fuck up more than just Andy Warhol, the magnate of modern pop art. You see, Andy wasn't the focus of her rage. It was the artwork, the system behind it. Men. Men, men, fucking awful men. The act was fluid. The emotion was hardened. Calcified. It was her very own ball and chain. It was not her own rock to push up a mountain, or a hill, or up the steepest hill in New York (is there one?) only to witness it roll back down, the vision, the mania, the eroticism of the act, the existentialism, the absurdity of it all motivating Camus to write a book upon it in 1942 or whenever he wrote it - she wasn't doing it all so she could pontificate it, or align it with her SCUM Manifesto. The act itself was her manifestation of said MANIFESTO. She did live, she did not die, to cater to the whole live, die, repeat, schemata - do she did not die, and she did not repeat. She was meant to do this. It was laid out, not by some fucked notion of a greater power or destiny, it was as she made it happen. She chose to, and she did. The politeness that may have come forth, the regret, is only enforced because that is what is expected and a woman so wayward, so feral, so rabid, deserved to be free. I am not attacking Warhol, as this is not about Warhol, it is about something very simple, and inherently crucial to her actions that day. "The struggle itself towards the heights is enough to fill a man's heart. One must imagine Sisyphus happy." – no, he isn't happy, he is pissed off, he worked his arse off, battled elements, emotions that not one man should bear, and he smiles at the end, fuck that, fuck you, Camus. That is what Valeries was making a point of. Action has reaction and repercussions, and though they can be seen through many different lenses, the only lens that truly matters is her own, and those who have luckily been given a chance, that and a choice, to decide to view like through her mirror darkly, are better for it.

"Valerie. Thank you for sitting down with me today, on the JERRY COCKADOODLE DANDY Show," *Solanas turns into Solanos, and she pulls from her crotch – something? - eyes rolling up into her head as the – WEAPON? THE GUN ITSELF? – passes through her pubic hair, and some part of the – WEAPON? THE GUN ITSELF? – brushes her slowly enlarging clitoris – Jerry felt his own cock struggle to not doodle in anticipation for – THE WEAPON? THE GUN ITSELF? – when she didn't carry on her person any form of weapon or object to execute her emotions, she was far too smart for that, though often her rage was passed off as merely that, woman's rage created by being ON! – the blob of the month (IS IT THE WEAPON? IS IT THE BLEEDINNG PUSSY?) - she had been granted an opportunity to be seen by millions of viewers, to silence the "IS IT A WEAPON?" types of remarks – and what she did was she pulled free, a copy of her latest MANIFESTO, entitled... THE WEAPON? THE GUN ITSELF? No, just these words... SCUM!*

Preach, Preacher-MAHN! Preach for us. We need to hear those words, re-read, over and over and over – so we may applaud the words of a once wise man who had little to no clue what he had created way back when, when we didn't refer to the periods as AD or BC or BBC (big black cock, oooo that is naughty, or BBC? ... neither you fool, so run, run, run now for fear I might slap you with the wettest of fish) all because a man of good means did something kind, occasionally. He fucked the local nutcase, as her pussy was tight, and looking after a mad woman, no matter what sees a man in good local stead, and the stories his sexually diseased whore of mother told, taken over by some odd delusion that she had birthed a son of this thing called, god, only she said dog, because at the time of describing this event that did not happen, she pointed at a dog, to which he husband Jospeh shook his head, smiling at her absurdity, only she pronounced it God, due to her sexually diseased mouth, dehydrated, cotton-mouthed, furry with that lovely white stuff called thrush. All of this came from that one scene. Greater scenes and wars and delusions have also been created because one bloke thought it would be good to record these events, as nobody would believe them, would they? Oh boy, if he had known, I think he might have just said, Fuck that, because at the end of the day, the guy would never be credited for documenting it, and all that was written, evolved, built upon would lose the core of his initial idea, which was to document the life of a local Jerusalem slumbum and the mates and kooks he met whilst he lived there. What would Valerie think about all this? She would, I can only imagine, look up into the eyes of this writer, and state, "David, is that you? I thought you might have travelled far with your Father, but not this far, fuck, not this far into obscurity."

Valerie wouldn't have liked me. Because I am first, a man. And I do understand her resentment of men. Resentment that transmogrified into loathing. You see, loathing is a very passive act. When hating, oh boy, we hate. This passivity allowed her to, not look up to, but try and wheedle her way into certain male dominated functions and scenes, to try and take advantage. Valerie was reversing the polarity of things to come, and that had sadly already been sealed in amber. Valerie took in men, because she needed the money. She once ejected a man, a child, a boy. David. Who she never saw again. Rejecting the male sex meant she was rejecting, not her past, but the whole notion of maleness. I think she also hated that she birthed a male, though if she were to birth a female she would have been as shrewd towards such a life than that of a wee baby boy. She knew it was best to shun the male. They are and will always be fixtures in a woman's life. Woman were created to take our load and process the life of the male's heir. Any form of ownership was null/void. "Life" in this "society" being, at best, an utter bore and no aspect of "society" being at all relevant to women, there remains to civic-minded, responsible, thrill-seeking females only to overthrow the government, eliminate the money system, institute complete automation and eliminate the male sex." *The male, both as sex, and the male sex, our genitals. So many times, she took us in, the male, and our appendages, and was paid (perhaps a pittance, perhaps not) for the luxury of man using a woman, HER, HERSELF, THE VALERIE SOLANAS, for all she is made to feel she is worth – a quick bump, thrust, and wet warm cavern to shoot our load up like pissing up a back alley. She rejected the sperm. The action. The derogatory assault, that didn't need to be voiced into her lower lip as they forgot the rule of no kissing. She hated men because men had always been that – MALE, extremely, unequivocally hetero-male.*

Solanas should
have tried harder
FUCK YOU
WARHOL!
the third shot
is the Devils
answer

PART III

TOO MANY BLOCKBUSTERS. TOO MANY SUPERHEROS. TOO MANY WHIPPED BITCHES THAT MAKE THE FANBOY DIRE. TOO LITTLE VISION. THERE IS VISION, HIDDEN AWAY IN CERTAIN CREATORS, YES, <u>OF COURSE THERE IS</u>, BUT THERE IS ALWAYS A <u>BUT</u> AND A COUNTER <u>ARGUMENT</u> THAT NEEDS REPRESENTATION; OTHERWISE WE MIGHT JUST HAVE THE CASE GO THE OTHER WAY, AND WE CANNOT ALLOW THAT, NOW, CAN WE?

YES/NO/MAYBE/WHO THE FUCK CARES? THERE ARE SYSTEMS IN PLACE, VAST EMPIRICAL TOWERS, ODDLY SHAPED LOGOS, EMBOSSED LEATHER DESK BLOTTERS MESSING THE WHOLE INFRASTRUCTURE. BUT NOT TO THE STANDARDS OF... THE TRUE AUTEURS. THE TRUE AUTEURS resulting in the true amateurs.

AMATEURS REPLACING TRIED AND TESTED AND POPULAR FACES AND FILMMAKERS.

Ridley looks over at Neil. Puffs on his cigar. Chomps down on it. Tastes that glorious immortal taste of oncoming lung-cancer. **Chomp! Chomp! Chomp!** – add in a plethora of cigar induced sloppy do-not-inhale-second hand smoke effected mouth squelches and rasps and **ONLY-SMOKERS-CAN-HEAR-AND-UNDERSTAND**-types of noises.

Neil: *Must you be here?*

Ridley chomps.

Neil: Was it not enough that you postponed my film by six years? Why are you here?

Ridley chomps, trying to keep down his tics.

Neil: Ridley, honestly stop with all that cigar specific noise, it is making me feel woozy. Anyway, I'm still surprised you're alive.

Ridley continues puffing on his cigar.

Accentuating and clarifying Neil's surprise and incredulity.

What Neil doesn't know won't hurt him. Nor make him jealous. *I puff on these for a reason kid,* Ridley thought to himself.

"This spaceship sucks. It's too..." the clone of Sigourney Weaver stopped herself mid-sentence... **"it is just too, too, well, like duh, like everything else out there, it is too space-shippie!"** the clone of Sigourney then stamped her foot.

"Someone please put her back into the growth pod for another twenty odd minutes!" Neil cries out - his South African accent threatening to be a problem.

"Why?" shrugs one of his production assistants.

"Why? Sigourney is only six years old!"

"So, not my problem. What does that even mean? I shouldn't ask her out on a date yet?"

"No, you forker!"

"Is that South African for Fucker, boss?"

"Where's Sharlto?"

Ridley stiffens.

Neil senses his rigidity.

"Where is Sharlto, Ridley?"

"Last I saw of him was... Fuck you, thank you, fuck you very much. That's right! He was going to jump into tight Lycra with all those fucking dots on him, and fuck you, fuck you very much so help me Napoleon, the last I saw of him was when his huge nut-sack was left staring at me"- that was all Ridley was willing to provide.

"Oh, for fork's sake! I wish I stuck with that Robocop sequel!"

"Neil?"

"What?"

"Sharlto is ready!"

"For what?"

"To get into the Alien costume."

"Good. Finally."

Ridley smirks to himself.

Even though this was Blomkamp's Alien 5, the one film his fans and himself had been trying to get going for the past few years, Ridley still would get Final Cut, Theatrical Cut, over the project. And of course, the various Directors Cuts. Which meant he would replace every single frame, and the minutest of things that were going to be Neil-esque would be destroyed and replaced by Ridley's already 40 hours' worth of film coverage, for such an eventuality, and he would rename the film ALIEN: Paradise Lost.

Reborn.
Revolted.
Rebelled.
Cigar puffing twat!

IF A DIRECTOR COMES UP TO YOU, INDICATES FOR YOU TO DROP ONTO YOUR KNEES, AND HE UNZIPS HIS FLIES – WHAT DO YOU DO?

DO YOU BOOK AN APPOINTMENT FOR AN OFFICIAL SESSION ON HIS COACH? OR DO YOU JUST MANIFEST THE INTERNAL

METHOD ACTOR, AND GO TO A MAGICAL PLACE, BEFORE PICKING UP THAT STIFFENING COCK AND GIVE THE DIRECTOR HEAD LIKE HE HAS NEVER HAD HEAD BEFORE?

THEN WHAT HAPPENS?

DO YOU SWALLOW HIS FUTURE RUGRATS DOWN YOUR THROAT AND THINK TO YOURSELF OBSESSIVELY, THIS IS ONLY A FILM PRODUCTION TASK, THIS IS ONLY A FILM PRODUCTION TASK, FIGHTING AGAINST YOUR NATURALLY SENSITIVE GAG-REFLEX, THE GAG JUST

MAKING THE EXPECTANT HORNY CUNT PLAY TONSIL JOUSTING WITH HIS MEATY AND UNWASHED APPENDAGE, AS YOU TRY TO FORM A NARRATIVE TO BETTER SWALLOW THIS BLEACHY, CUMMY, SALTY SUBSTANCE?

A SUBSTANCE YOU START BREAKING DOWN INTO ITS

COMPONENT PARTS - THINKING, SEMEN, SWIMMING, SEMEN, FIGHTING, SEMEN, HEADING TOWARDS MY TONSILS, THE BACK OF MY THROAT, ALL SWIMMING TO REACH AN EGG THAT YOUR FUCKING BODY DOES NOT HAVE FOR THEM TO SLAPDUNK THEMSELVES INTO AND CHILL OUT FOR NINE-

MONTHS UNTIL THEY ARE YET ANOTHER FUCKING MOUTH TO FEED IN THIS FUCKED UP WORLD OF OURS - AS IF THAT IS FUCKING NORMAL, ALL BECAUSE YOU HOPE THAT LATENT HOMOSEXUAL PERVERT AUTEUR WILL LATER PRODUCE YOUR HORROR MOVIE SCRIPT? GET A GRIP! YOU FUCKING MORON!

We slept together. Under the stars. The crashing space station didn't change our plans to fuck, lick, moisten each other. As it crashed a good few clicks away, we stopped our sexual frenzy and let the ripple effect move our bodies closer. Madonna praised us with some limerick smattered with disco funk and an oddly MHz punk solo cut in, randomly. The explosion reached the skies, the strength of the blast pushing the "Nothing to see here, God" – clouds out of the way. The heat slammed us together and picked us up as one. I wrapped my legs around my lover's hips. He did the same. And we were lifted, and what felt like levitation that went on for days but was no doubt a mere inflection in our final seconds together, the way the universe works in these moments of death, time undulates and expands – sensations are pricked up, far more heightened. And we did our dance, slow dancing in the eye of a ripple of aftershock and debris and twisted heated metal and liquid slashes that could only have been melted glass – embedding itself into us in this maelstrom – embedding and hardening, becoming diamonds in our backs, thighs and we just spun around, we felt nothing but our two bodies, as they were before the aftershock and violent tsunami of space station debris – slow, sensuous, as if on some gimbal, a spinning turntable – listening to the music of Madonna and we spun. When the moment was to end, everything sped up... into a dizzying chaos that made me cum prematurely and made his dick wilt, no longer threatening my umbilical bay with his huge knob end. We died together. We exploded into shards together. We combined our matter and would live on in perpetuity, perhaps in later life brushed by archaeological experts, distinguishing us, the queer lovers of 1950, in the middle of Texas, killed by a space station that had never been listed or televised – a NASA secret, a secret advancement that they knew would progress, but wouldn't make the news, not until it had reached perfection and the public would accept such a grand fete, that of a vast space station. Something torn from the pages of pulp sci-fi comics – that would, divinely fall apart – and destroy another secret, tear into it, shred it, and expand them, and mingle them, in ways they could never have imagined, and it was an acceptance of the universe. A higher sign of a union. A secret covering and ending another clandestine, pure thing; secrets upon secrets, delivered, destroyed, and revived in power ways – a love between two very much in love homosexual men - it combined with us – these two ex-military men that secured their gates at NASA, allowing us to express and combine – genetically and spiritually - forming us into a much larger secret. The secret of the gay military servicemen drafted into NASA's security duty – we were allowed to become part of something bigger than us, as a paired unit, two gay lovers - becoming part of history whilst no one ever knew of our histories. The dead do speak. That is where I am. Where we are. We are one. Combined. The station isn't, don't be fucking idiotic. The station was a nexus event. And we are the results. We are the reason certain Angels in Graveyards altered. The forlorn, head in their hands angels started to shift, peek out between their fingers. They started to rise their cement crafted eyes; their slouch was gradually through the generations onwards from this event rising. Eyes cast upward, not in praise of God, but in utter denial of God. Their forms for generations that represent untimely deaths have been miscommunicated/misinterpreted. It represents something alternative to the old ways of the Church. Before the word gay and meaning of it was labelled and marked out as sin and something to hide, these angels didn't have their face in a hand, looking downcast, in regret and sorrow, and confusion. They were up, in the air, not smiling, but placid in their executions. When sodomy was not sodomy but merely two males making love or hate fucking one another, working through what this meant for them as human beings, these angels were not crestfallen or in despair. They were just as accepting of the notion of male on male, female on female love and sexual expression. We created the angels eventual rise from their fucking makers messed up forlorn forms. They were Angels of love, not untimely death. It was only the thoughts, attitudes and politics that got into them and their makers, expressing something they had no awareness of, but worked towards making an example of, and sadly was sidelined for the Church, in remembrance of an untimely death. A weeping angel weeps because of the mistakes of the Church and all religions. They can now take shape, whether through animating themselves or the craftsman, the sculptors, and artificers have sensed a change. We created that. We do not want thanks. Admire the explosion, Admire the cause and the effect. Live as you want to live, not dictated by social or familial pressures. Be you. The total you. Fuck in a field and die a death but feel comforted that these events have greater ripples and casualties than you could ever imagine. Flowers with the most vibrant of colours turn the most rustic of environments pure and beneficial. Isn't that what love is? Making the blasé omnipotent? We are God. We are our own God. We control our lives when the moment is right. We just need to believe more.

In truer and better things, so help us none of the gods we have be conned, indoctrinated into believing in. We disperse now. We go onward. We must. We need to. We create by moving the language we were assigned at birth, and we break into to it. It is fluid, but it is not liquid.

Did that cut go deep? Is it now a wound? Let me treat it with this salve, with this saying, **Sticks and stones may break my bones, but words will never hurt me.** *Well, dear all-seeing, all-knowing person, who might later be an actual individual or a mere metaphor, this is not a broken bone or mere bruising, no mere scab, or graze... this is years of words breaking into the already infected zone, perpetually contributing to the wound and creating a wider gap – words do not tumble out, they stay, interweave themselves into the wound - never sealing closed. So, apply those words, go on, because the* **sticks** *will be one stitch, come undone by another criticism, or observation, which it is usually passed off as, sealed in a blasé, airy-fairy dismissiveness – no big thing, just an observation, just an insight – no, it is not, you are being one mean cunt - as the attackers like to believe they are offering us, mere words that can help or better ourselves, constructive criticism is a fine art that not many have learnt to shape and make easier to swallow – especially those we assign to being our protectors and loved ones - the* **stones** *will be a couple more stiches, and the stitches will pull themselves off with reckless abandon and cause extreme pain, and as per, increasing the hurt, increasing the pressure to unburden oneself to try and distance themselves and reinforce in their minds that it is the physical the hurts the most, not words, empty things, words cannot harm you – no, that is true, but not* *in certain circumstances, especially when coming from certain figures in your life – the stiches are torn, not peeled, ripped away, and still, that phrase, that great saying, that great combative retort to bullies, it is fucking pathetic and has no basis. There is no Paracelsus here. We do not need to protect ourselves, when the people that have caused this pain, are meant to be the protecters – still, weaponise this phrase, this saying, this line of words that counteract, and whose poison seeps into another poison, only to create an alchemical reaction that further brings you to the ground, shaving away facial growth off the sharp flint and rocks and grit – a shield, a retort, from words they are not ushering in, like a high-viz jacketed builder, ensuring that the truckload of materials are safely reversed onto the work site, but that they scything through me and many of my generation and the generations before me and before them, wearing us down. This ointment, this phrase, these words to counter-act other words, it is all futile. Words do hurt, and the more we try to minimalise the effects and affects of words, the more we will ache, and never properly heal.*

The fuck you list. The fuck you list we all have in our heads. The fuck you list that exists inside and has never been verbalised. When it has it been, sadly it has delivered nothing. We create for ourselves a paradox of contradictions. It seems by swearing, screaming, sharing it, not enough people listen, or that not enough people actually listen and process it and break it down as we wish for it to be seen and heard as. It needs to be shared, not halved, it needs to be witnessed, it needs to be felt. When we process these feelings, these events, the agonies, the memories, and yes the traumas, it is always a mutated edge of the original issue, and usually aimed at somebody who has no reason to be on the end of your jousting staff – by enacting upon those repressed emotions, we create something for ourselves that doesn't encourage a full and total obliteration, as that isn't human and that isn't real. By doing so, only reinforces the fact that these individuals have harmed you, and that they have only furthered something unobtainable. You can't get rid of it. But you can share it. You can hope people will read the names and then shout, or whisper, or think, as a collective of thinkers and artists and non-artists, fuck you. Together, we can pressure these arseholes, by a shared id, a shared mantra, a shared fuck you, maybe to give them food for thought. To stop them and have them think upon their actions. That, or feel paranoid that the world is ready to pull them up on their nonsense and ways. Say it with me, Fuck you!

I was up late last night, anticipating the usual irritable leg syndrome I get when fighting my meds, and the strange sensation of sleep being brought forward, offered as an extra to this thing called existence – time to clock out – time to unnaturally fall into a deep sleep, and wake myself up chortling like a pig in shit – trying to figure out if I have sleep apnea - my medication, always referred to as my "sleeping-pills" make me feel hungry, giving over to a headiness, a grogginess, a lofty, totally freeing release from the pangs of reality – usually swiftly followed by an insatiable hunger that has contributed in the past few years to my weight gain – that and I am a greedy fuck – I fucked off the sheep counting and instead tried to, not count, but go through all the people on my fuck you list; though it didn't inspire sleepiness, if anything else it forced me awake, it gave me a greater idea to immortalise and extract the fuck you list from myself – alongside all those tied feelings to said fuck you list occupants.

So, here I go.

In no order:

Liane - *Fuck you!*

Darren – *Fuck you!*

Marion – *Fuck you!*

Bob – *Fuck you!*

Austin- *Fuck you!*

Sven – *Fuck you!*

Fred – *Fuck you!*

Max – *Fuck you!*

Keeley – *Fuck you!*

Rayy – *Fuck you!*

Holly – *Fuck you!*

Josh – *Fuck you!*

Jason – *Fuck you!*

Ricky- *Fuck you!*

Richard - *Fuck you!*

Rae- *Fuck you!*

Melenie – *Fuck you!*

Julia- *Fuck you!*

Callum – *Fuck you!*

Vicky – Fuck you!

Simon – *Fuck you!*

Jack- *Fuck you!*

Another Jack- *Fuck you!*

James – *Fuck you!*

Lloyd – *Fuck you!*

Jack - (yes, another) – *Fuck you!*

Kirby - *Fuck you!*

Lu - *Fuck you!*

Sophie - *Fuck you!*

Faith - *Fuck you!*

Rhianon – *Fuck you!*

Drew – *Fuck you!*

Amy -*Fuck you!*

Chlo – Fuck you!

Sadie - *Fuck you!*

Maths Teacher who locked me in a classroom and went on a long spiel about how I will amount to nothing– *Fuck you!*

Homophobic History Teacher Mr. Brazier – *Fuck you!*

Every single police officer I have had to deal with – *Fuck you all!*

Rosie – *Fuck you!*

George – *Fuck you!*

Sam – *Fuck you!*

Taylor – *Fuck you!*

Alex – *Fuck you!*

A waitress who worked at the local Deli who always referred to me as a freak when I wasn't there – *Fuck you!*

Lewis – *Fuck you!*

Another Jack – *Fuck you!*

Manus – *oh boy fuck you, you snivelling talentless pointless worm!*

Ewan – *Fuck you!*

Lewis, yes, another one – *Fuck you!*

Dan – *Fuck you!*

Sarah – *Fuck you!*

Tash - *Fuck you!*

Terese – *Fuck you!*

Stevie – *Fuck you!*

Wade – *Fuck you!*

Ollie – *Fuck you!*

Olly – *Fuck you!*

Marg – *Fuck you!*

Rick - *Fuck you!*

Helen - *Fuck you!*

Ellis – *Fuck you!*

Andrea – *Fuck you!*

Andy – *Fuck you!*

Sheila – *Fuck you!*

Every YMCA or Supported Living Worker – *Fuck you!*

The Local Council – *Fuck you!*

John - *Fuck you!*

Jake – *Fuck you!*

Muggy Mikey – *Fuck you!*

Josh, yes, another one – *Fuck you!*

Shady Ade – *Fuck you!*

All the noisy neighbours I had whilst at GWM – *Fuck you!*

Jody – *Fuck you!*

Another Jodie – *Fuck you!*

Betty – *Fuck you!*

Paul – *Fuck you!*

Max, yes, another one – *Fuck you!*

Brian – *Fuck you!*

Erika – *Fuck you!*

Ben - *Fuck you!*

Another Ben – *Fuck you!*

Lily – *Fuck you!*

Lilian – *Fuck you!*

Libby – *Fuck you!*

Mitze – *Fuck you!*

Amy – *Fuck you!*

Zachary – *Fuck you!*

Kevin – *Fuck you!*

Bradley – *Fuck you!*

Garett – *Fuck you!*

Lauren – *Fuck you!*

Alice - *Fuck you!*

Helen, yes, another one – *Fuck you!*

Helen's freaky, OTT, mouthy mate – *Fuck you!*

Fuck you!

All of you.

Say it with me. Say the names aloud, lure their names onto your tongue and release it, and then deliver each fuck you! – with all of the suppressed rage you have mollycoddled, when it should have been unleashed, naked, raw without question freed to hopefully lose its weight before retuning to plague your brainstem(s), and tackle the inherent injustices with those two words – *fuck you!*

And to all the other's I have been hurt by,

FUCK

YOU!

5

Wall. Eyes. Giggling. Pointed fingers. Giggling. Red brick, but not the old kind. Wall. Balcony. Aids infested Steve. Stormy Normie. Weird. Need. Do it! Concentrate. Death. Do it or what could happen? Eyes. Done it. Still not right. No composure. Mania. Obsessive. Compulsive. Matt Lucas. Sex. Queer. Fat. Sexy. Want to have sex with him. Joke. Dark humour. Made victim. Abused. Bullied. Obsessive. Understand me please? Half-naked me. Eyes. Mockery. Fence. Cat. Dog. Judgement. Misunderstanding. Obsessions. Ritual. Habits. Spit. Making noises. Mocked. Alone. Free. Not so free. Trapped. Nowhere to go to express. Shower. Turn on. Make noises. Tic. Stim. Perform. Accentuate. Spastic. Me. Freak. Me. Ritualisation. Performance. Not a dance but a gyration. A full body meltdown. Spit. TV being wiped down. Golden child, replacing a stillborn son, and being merely a disappointment. Brighton. Newhaven. John. Mental warfare. Abuse. Bullying. Triggering. Fat. Look like this ugly guy on this show, calls me Tyrone. Mum shares John's words. Shares his oddities. VHS only. DVD only. Cry because no VHS. ANNOYED as no special features on DVD. Go to Blu-ray. Yes. HDMI, not there. Same as DVD. HDMI there, TV too small.

College. Bad. School bad. Infants school, not brilliant, but better. Nursery, fun. Living. Life. Still some assholes littered in their like bad seeds. Son. No son. Baffled. Confused. Paul Merton lookalike, apparently. Unskilled. Stagnant dreams produce sulphuric atmospheres that had been captured in thick cannisters – releasing the damned plague would cause eye-explosions – dropping off dicks – extremely low hanging vulvas – dragging like chain and ball - the shared vision of the two little angels turned Nazi sympathisers – turned into tissue paper – no matter how you roll it on the work surface, the art board, the cork board, the canvas, the A4 sheet of paper or card, the little Nazi angels survive – Nazis come to mind when you think bomb, Germany, sausage, schnitzel, and even when having photographic evidence placed in front of you, of two little boys, gas masks strapped on, looking off to the right, to the horizon, you automatically think of Nazis – or I do – I have a fetish for the wardrobe – it is iconographic – evocative – staying – it has staying power – these visions damning every single person on this planetoid called – home.

BROWNIE
TARGET
SIX-20

a million stagnant dreams

It is in our nature to panic.

Especially when it concerns our dreams.

Panic not.

These dreams are meant to be used as signposts.

Signposts to lead you away from them.

The dream doesn't wish to trick you into circling back into the dream-illogicality-centre.

It wants you to detach yourself from it, as the dream isn't weighing you down, you yourself are weighing the dream down.

INNER
SPACE
THIS IS A
DANGEROUS
PLACE
BECAUSE
THERE IS
NOTHING
HERE
STOP
panic
do not
panic
shrunken
withered
dreams

Useless. Go to the shops. Stories about my idiocy. Not true, some true, but I take them and embellish the bad parts all to make a comedic example of it all. Tics. Not tics. Can't read. Can read. You know too much about films, whereas people just watch them - no one is interested. I want to say, are you that uncultured and dumb? after all the BBC Radio 4 shows you listen to, you stupid mean old cunt. Old. Dying. Not. Yet. Dead. Death. Morning. Afternoon. Lunch. Dinner. Fat. Foot smells. Food consumption. Pocket money. Books. Books. Books. Books. Films. Films. Films. Catered to. Catered to because that is the only thing he can sit still for. Smoking. Hate it. Love it. Need it. Vape it. Do not vape it. Pillar to post. Rapid. Awhirl. Still stupid. Rushed botched editorial job. Crap covers. Bad books. Awful human. Jerk. Asshole. Justice. SJW hater and supporter. Poet of digital means. Poet of shart. A wet fart. Sweating. Diabetes. Wish upon a star for me to have never been created, cheers mum, love you too. *Not*! Bullying. Harassment. Violence. Black Eyed Peas, a song called Shut up just shut up, not the actual title, the only lyrics that stay with me, as I am/was gaffer taped to a chair, gagged, bound. Meteorites will kills us. Scared. Obsessed. Can't watch DINOSAURS the movie on VHS anymore. So scared. Of myself. Of my brain. What I have inside. Attacked. Abused. Fight back. Get labelled a woman beater. I get locked up when I was defending myself.

Scratches. Crotch kicked. Black and blue and purple eyes. I am not violence and violence is not me. I am violent and violence is all I can be. Violence with words, but not fists. I am weak. I am broad and capable, but I don't wish to be. I want to have a bigger dick. A smaller dick. No dick. I want to be a woman. I want to be an animal. I want the life of a pampered pooch. I want a job. I need a job. My job is to exist. Life is hard work as it is. Money is evil. Money is great. Books released with no theatrical displays. Shove it out – take the methodology of a council estate slag – go on, push the little fucker out – lend more waste to the land. I am rattled. I am cage, who is shaking me up, piss off you fucking melt. Lipstick smears around a cock I used to know and own. Building building. Typos. Errors. Editorial discrepancies. Devolving. Evolving. Typos. Errors. Errors. Typos. The typo-method. The error-method. Editorial mutilation. The editor is a butcher and a fiend. So, I decide not to be. Allow your messiness to breathe. Children, breathe. Books breathe. Music, screech. Typos and errors. Errors and typos. Do not mistake our admittance to failure as an easy opening to try and kick us, because we are sadistic, masochistic bastards and will proffer certain parts of our body – of work – of physical meat – to aim for and to harm. Beat us up. Beat us off. Trickling cum so beautiful, when aged, and having marinated in the bottom of your shaft – peaking up from the ball-trenches, thinking, is it time, nope – is it time – erection and arousal makes sure the egg is secured and quarantined by your genetics and contributing to bastardising all that was you. Men penetrate with cock and egg. When the woman doesn't want your grubby seed in them, and they just wanted a moments release, you take advantage you filthy boar of a man – fuck you, men – language timothy, fuck off you cunt – the system of language, of release, of performance has encouraged my writing – yet, every time I go to record I am inhibited – there is nowhere to release so powerfully - and even then, they never get satisfied, do they? – the poor lass has to finish herself off – in cunt and in spirit. Cunt is a beautiful word. Tasty. Ripe. Foul. Foal. Fowler, stop picking at it, you'll make it worse. Eat the book. Suckle the letters. Let the words melt on your brain tongue. Mental dissatisfaction is the key to all of this that we create for ourselves. Brutal. Bullish. Boring. Onto the next channel. Hop. Scotch. Entresol with lavish tiles and obsessively cleaned with the best and most unharmful chemical products. A gallery looking down, from all three sides, onto the staircase, the foyer, the entrance – those double doors, brass, oak, thick, affirmed, royalist in their orchestration. I do not cut up, so shut up! I cut up on page. Word salad has been used to attack and vilify. Well, word salad isn't a bad thing, only, salad is distasteful, and I think the word, the phrases, the work deserves a distasteful reputation, but word salad implies a hodgepodge of things, that are meant to be good for you. It isn't word salad; it is a buffet of junk. Word buffet. Junk word buffet. Word Scramble. Word Refuse. Death to word salad. Death to the WORD and all its good or bad intentions. Gaelic languages make me hard. Evectional contributions to the hardened personality. The rocket from *Le voyage dans la lune* lodged into the back of our heads. Open mic-live and the spoken word poet stands there sweating and thinking, *oh boy, I can't poetically justify my being here, so instead just adlib,* and thus was created a standup comedian with delusions of poetic status. The poet came first. Poetry is more than just flowery words, it is activistic. Activism is inlaid. Poetry that is political is all if not most poetry. Poetry is manifesto manifested in gestures and performance. School's do not preach the good name of poetry in performative terms, which is just wrong. You are always distanced by the academicians' methods of education. The Lord of the Flies, brilliant book, but when forced to study, it loses itself. Poetry, nah, no thanks. I love them musicality of John Cooper Clarkes work, the no-holds-barred power of his rhyming. Publishers defaming rhyme annoys me – let the performative transgress. Putting *fuck* or *cunt* into a poem isn't transgressive, but the act of shouting it, whispering it, performing it is. Create the scene. Reading poetry, it is subjected to your own internal poetical muse/identity/nub of poetically confused wants and aspirations. I have a poet, an activist, a spokesperson, a spoken word identity hidden inside me, but the more important question is... have you?

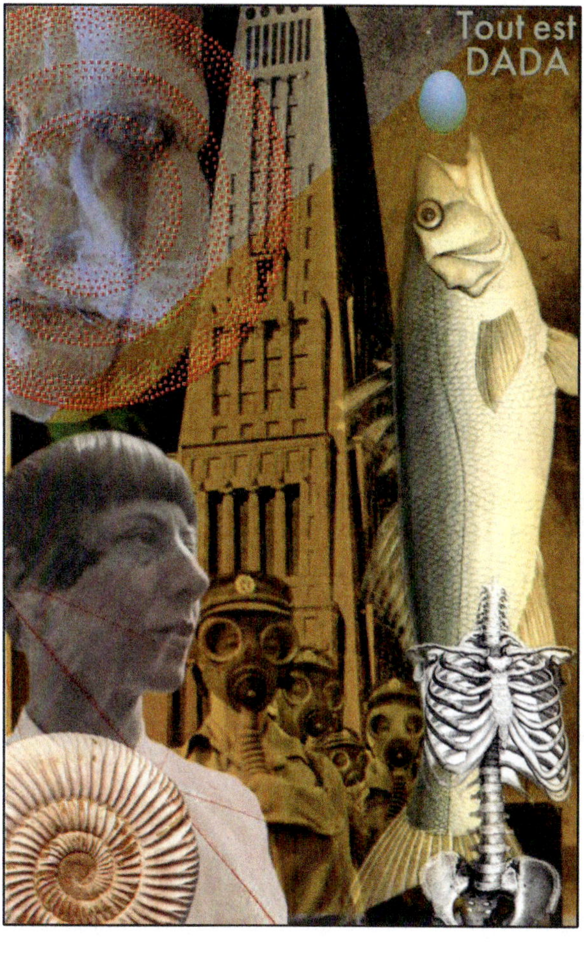
Tout est
DADA

Dada is the first word most children say. Dada. Dada. Dada. The Dad cluelessly coos and encourages for more. *Is Dada not enough for you? Impatient prick!* Mother looks on – at you, through you, penetrating you (makes a change) and you try to not avert your gaze to meet hers – there she is, in all of her glory, from the corner of your eye, from the corners of this established link between you, her, and the dear baby. Dada. Not Dad-ah! Dada. We always assume that it is an abbreviation for Daddy. No, your child is an avant-garde master in the making, so start paying more attention to this child. Their brains are like Dada art being confirmed in the flesh. They are piecing together the vastly erratic waves, colours, curvatures to the world around them. The source is thick, bold, there are bright colours because it is the inherent Dadaist inside of them. Taking the brash, gaudy bauble of experience, only to attribute it to an inverted sense of reality that they have pieced together on the behalf of other Dadaists in the making, and by/for themselves. Pay attention to the *goo-goo gah-gahs* you pointless pillocks. They are not mere baby comments and expressions, they are broken down phrases, garbled milk juiced sayings from *their* future selves. Your child isn't creating a **<u>collage</u>** because it has yet to develop its fine art skills. *Collage* is peak transformation for many and all artists. Take the philosophies of photography that *Sontag* espoused and moaned on and on about in her 1970s mini book (that felt like reading a longer version of WAR & PEACE) ON PHOTOGRAPHY and throw it out. The prose is very wayward, but not in a fun way, and it is hard to *tune* into her particular verbiage. The pleonasm is driven into your chest, spread like a venomous bite, *the* poison seeping in, but instead of appreciating that warm injection of an - other being's tastes and *linguistic* style, sad to say, you are kind of infiltrated to the point that you just want to stop. The *monotony* of subjects and manner *of* repeating the same thing, over, and over, with additional filler, to bulk the essays and *the* topic. The book is whimsical in the sense it is dry, and unrelatable. The choice of words, quotes, the *execution* was frustrating – it provided an opening, that never fully delivered, I am *still hoping* for a sequel to it, *to get* some form of identity, *outside* of her prose and the voice and character *of Susan Sontag* that she has created. It is *because* her vantage on photography is not my own, and the less said about her decision to leave *her opinions* at the door, or to randomly, tic like inject it, leaves you wanting either/or – tread it in, Susan, *go on* - all that opinion bursting to be expressed, *only to be mopped up* in your wake – like a dog owner following the dog trailing *in* their own shite, baby wipe, scrubber at the ready, *bucket* hanging around your neck by its handle, *water* sloshing, but never landing on the effected zones – tread that opinion in like a proud dog does *with its own shit* - into the book space. The modern-day *usage of* photography has *evolved.* The collage is making the concrete fluid. Incorporating the fluid into your own cement mix. Your own plaster to reform and revise. The *collage* is made from scraps. From photos and art already assigned a place. Photographs capture moments in time, but they are often captured with an artistic intention. Take away that veneer and sand it down and what do you have? Scraps, scraps, and more scraps. Piece said scraps together and what do you get? Art-in-the-making. Art-in-the-un-making. It isn't about mere documentation; it is now about the weaponisation of said image. Used to cancel, to destroy, to mock, to goad, to sell, to force protests or force rebellion or to force the usual knee-jerky standard of rebellion, typing shit up on social media platforms behind fake names and overly filtered avatars. The most honest person on social media is the person who is not using such platforms. We all have different identities for different environments and people. Different friends for different seasons and reasons. We are weaponizing the weapon, and the ill/or well-intended use of said images are being recreated. Do we ever make collage art out of other collages? No, not unless it is a collage of our own invention – a subversion will be had. Collaging collages, created by other people's collages to make our own collage. We treat the collage as sacred, but not the singular element and images as sacred. Weaponize the already ill-affecting weapon. The collage is an alternative reality, a new reality, and an impressively expressive medium. Some are great, some are good, some are terrible, some are pathetic. But, collage art, working within the collage medium and aesthetical outlines, the aesthetic of collage in of itself, the setup, the realm, the world, the collage art piece that isn't outside of the medium and aesthetical method and boundary – as a certain attitude, and place in modern art, historical art. The collage of a child is different to that of an adult, though some would like to think otherwise, meh, fuck them, and fuck you for even musing on that potentiality. Collage art isn't for children, it is for the modern thinkers the rebels, the retaliators, the restless, the absurd, the intellectuals, the fool, the well-meaning theoretician with little to no proof of his credentials. Tear the image, and tear again, scissor another, try and exact that agitation and unease and need to reform, redevelop, to recreate. We use collage because we are shit artists, not always, but mostly, we source, nip, tuck, explore, we admire the pieces, but know we can do more by it, by adapting, altering, enhancing, tear, release, get sticky, collage is messy, but some are so dedicated to the precision I get jealous and bored of the precision – no, that is a lie, I admire the precision, knowing I am not as well informed on it, because I believe to follow the herd of one, yourself. Create and express and collage and type and edit and photograph and draw and dance and film and paint and express, express, express as you want and try and blend, adapt, source, but sourcing isn't admission of unoriginality, it is the adject denial of unoriginality, it is a full blast of addition to having to be inspired and goaded into writing, drawing, filming, photographing; as we, you, and me, we must, he strive, we neglect, we forget, we lie to ourselves about constant stimulation of the arts – we need a source material, you need it, you have to admit to yourself that sources create originality. Nothing is original, and that in of itself is a creation of a new mode of expression. Bresson said, *"For me, filmmaking is combining images and sounds of real things in an order that makes them effective. What I disapprove of is photographing with that extraordinary instrument — the camera — things that are not real. Sets and actors are not real."* – the images are our actors and sets. I am sorry Bresson, the collage is not your method of expression. Or is it? All film is doing is collaging stills, frame by frame, at certain speeds and captured on certain lenses and ratios. We inject language and music and motion through colour, placement of image. We create our own movies – or, in fact our own movie posters. We create art through tailoring. Bresson also said, *"I'd rather people feel a film before understanding it,"* that is what Dada is. Was he a secret Dadaist? Feel it. Connect. Distance yourself so you can situate yourself in the best possible position to "get it", or do one better, to fucking well "feel it". The collage method is fluid, yet we somehow manage to retain that collage style, feel, texture, and appeal. Collage is not only a mode of construction and reconstruction, but also devastation. Destroying so something can become anew. You must kill before you can shed that singular tear, running down onto the three strands of hair - that makes one thick log – on your first child's head, stroking it, feeling the water, shaping it, curling it, wrapping it around your forefinger, musing on the death of art, the death of mother, stroking that strand, playing with it, the baby smells like warmth, future, the death of art's result, rubbing the water, the post Dada death art tear into the structure and hair follicle – until the hair is merely faded, yet you still play with it and stroke it, it is still there, muscle memory, hair memory, Dada, you just dissolved my hair, Dada, I am not saying Dad-ah, I am saying Dada, you killed the wrong person, you were meant to kill yourself. That is the point. To sacrifice yourself and throw yourself onto that pyre, and not somebody else. That is what creating a collage is. Sacrifice, opening yourself to suck in the flames, the bullets, the blades, the bombs, the blasts, the word, the images, the intonations, the aggravations, the shifts in earthly time and earthly evolution, to suck in the volatility, the violence, the harm, the abuse, the trauma, the smoke, the blood, the smut, the lovers, the liars, the criers, the words are not written because I feel the need to write around an image, I am writing to reinforce that notion, that ideal, I am typing to feel inspired, I am using images before the words, fully phrased and conceptualised, before formation on the mind-tongue, the literal tongue, shaped like clay or putty by the mouth, the tongue, the vocal chords doing a lot of work but hardly being illuminated in this bright bold exclamation of respect to the powers of vocal projections, that are enhanced and far more omnipotent when unspoken, and left to take on a violence, a striating, strobe effect, connected between the unsaid, the unknown, and the fully known and fully intended in your mental-mouth, readied to project onto a page, not into open space, but a space that will later be seen, heard, felt. Feel it. Collage is Prince Charles, when he was a Prince, mind you, he will forever be a Prince in my eyes, because, those names, those titles hold very little for me, apart from Princess Diana, she was the embodiment of a Princess, in modern terms, of course – where was I? Oh yes, our High-Knee, he is collage – what do I mean by that? I mean he is useless, unless framed, shot, positioned, and edited correctly. He is a tool for the government and for us. We have power to create such splendidly weird, odd, batshit scenarios, which is helped by his blunders, and his unusually rubbery, not so handsome face. Should we, do it? Though in many senses they are public figures, and in so many ways in the public domain for us to use as we please because, we the not-so-United-Kingdom pay for their luxuries, and why? Because it is tradition –

Tradition, tradition! Tradition! Tradition, tradition! Tradition!

- *The Fiddler on the Roof* lyric summarises

nothing in relation to the monarchy and royalist way – but, it is a good song, and lyrics wise, I can't be sued for its use here – can I? Okay it is not *TFOTR lyrics* (hastily looks about himself, in that extremely harried way men get about them when caught in a tricky situation, and they often resemble someone looking for a weapon or they look like they have lost their dog, used to its annoying presence under their feet twenty-four-seven) it is just me typing the word Tradition six times. Yes. I should really use more film stills in my collages and implement more colour. Then again, my style of dictated by my emotions and in all honesty, seeing collage art being done at an exceptional level, both physically, with various materials, and digitally, I might as well throw my hands up in frustration and admit defeat. I won't. This book will feature artwork, all collages by a man called Paul Warren, who is making quite a name for himself in the Indie Publishing scene. His artwork is unique, in that it is totally collage... Collage with a capital c. The colour, the precision, the way the eye takes it all in, a story in image form, but, still open for interpretation, open for dissection and personal analysis. The theme of this book is to rant, to rave, but to also execute it so that it isn't merely shrugged off or acknowledged as "oh, autofiction" or "oh, automatic writing" – stop, automatic writing is just writing, this is something else. I am channelling all past mistakes the world has made, and so should you, if you know what is good for you, my chummy-bum-chums! A manifesto is more than an agenda. It is more than Wikipedia describes it: **A manifesto is a written declaration of the intentions, motives, or views of the issuer, be it an individual, group, political party, or government.** (No, it isn't on the behalf of any form of politics, you tits, and it doesn't always have to be mired in politics, even though a lot of what I write about is claimed as working-class, labour-appreciation) **A manifesto usually accepts a previously published opinion or public consensus or promotes a new idea with prescriptive notions for carrying out changes the author believes should be made.** (Fuck yes, that is more like it!) **It often is political, social, or artistic in nature, sometimes revolutionary, but may present an individual's life stance. Manifestos relating to religious belief are generally referred to as creeds or confessions of faith.** (Snooze off, bible breath) I wish to take the manifesto into new horizons, where it isn't mere words projected onto page to try and amass a big enough crew who agrees or sees validation in my stances, my political upheavals, and artistic intentions. The manifesto can be fun, insightful, but I never want to abuse it, the whole format of it, no, I want to obliterate it, destroy it with an ideological scatology, a newfound method of expression, to allow people to not read between the lines, or take everything on as face value, even though that seems to be conning people out of what they expect from a manifesto – anyway, that is why I am here, to challenge, to absorb, to fragment, to warp, to stretch, to pull, to tug off (oi oi) pudgy flesh barnacles and serve them up to you, not in some fancy pants hotel or restraint but to offer it to you up a sleazy location and its most popular back alley for wheeling, dealing and fucking a time travelling Victorian era prostitute, who dissolves with each thrust, leaving an imprint – for the Time Police to save money on their chalk stock – that they use to outline a murder! – Time Police still unable to figure out who Jack the Ripper was. Stop you fucks! Hold on! Isn't there better things to get so Time Cop-y stroppy over and about? This is more than rant, it is more than articulate waffling/warbling, it is an autistic meltdown in overdrive, with no end, and if there is, I have no doubt it is affixed to something called – conformity. I shrug that off. Then I pick it back up, hold it up, and I transform it – it, that conformity and laugh in the face of it, spit flying, partially ruining what image it is or whatever the object so decides to be in my palms, in those select and no doubt specific moments - the notion, the image, the object, morphing into what it was all along... into a scrap of printed paper. It has a various fonts, sizes, headers, and popular names and strangely non-AI-generated celebrity images (they don't need any help from the Stable Diffusions 2.1's of the world, the celebs manage to make themselves look freakish and all kinds of fake, all by their not so lonely, yet still extremely secluded selves) and we witness the start of something. It is physical, tangible, and as close as we will ever get to touching the likes of Timothy (jailbait) Cham-a-lamb-a-lama-lay, Brad Pitt, Ryan Gosling, Anna De Armas, Ben Affleck, Anthony Hopkins, and the only time that we will be that close to millions of pounds – via the printed image. That is our tool. We need glue. We need surfaces. Then, without them we can use our computer savviness to create digital art – and there, at a click of a button we have images galore. *Manifestum* is Latin, obviously Latin, and so sensual, and so erotic. *Manifestum*. Manifesting our manifesto with images. The anti-collage brigade think we are dim, unoriginal and thieves. They probably would even be stupid enough to accuse us of not knowing what Manifestum means/is. The smarter party always aims to knock you down, and in the process showing themselves up, in all their high and mightiness – for, in what I assume they assume of us is that we are as slow as those children that make "pretty pictures" and their first real go at "art" – notice the "" back there? – those special collages in pre-school. How rude and dismissive of the capabilities of a child's mind. My assumption of their assumption is presumptuous, but there is nothing but truth there. For all we know, us morons - that we are seen as being - grown men and woman stuck in the years of our childhood, sticking pieces of tissue paper and stickers all over a piece of not so durable card – we are the simplified and stupid of the artworld; ignorance, that is all it is. *Manifestum* is what it is; yet, still, they will undermine us, and if we reply with, "Scio quid sit Latinum, et multiplicibus linguis versatus sum, tibi gratias ago valde." - they will still believe they are above us, telling us that what we said, in answer, and what we produced wasn't Latin, but our take on a language we could never understand – not seeing the flaw in their denunciations and negative vibe being thrown over us like some weird anti-fire blanket – Manifesto sounds like Manifestum, and still we the dullards, the deluded, the idiots, are stuuuuuuuuuuuuuuuuuuuuuuuuuuuuuuuu uuuuuuuuuuuuuuuuuuuuuuuuuuuuuuuuuu uuuuuuuuuuuuuuuuuuuuuuuuuuuuuuuuuu uuuuuuuuuuuuuuuuuuuuuuuuuuuuuuuuuu pid! – if you want to make an argument that we are stupid and merely guessing, guess correctly yourselves! We are the paper and scissor and miniature scalpel wielders – those who can only mimic others' works (supposedly) – which is inaccurate – we are assumed that we couldn't read that, nor anything that has some bougie aura around it – like French words/ nor have the capabilities of being thinkers, readers, or capable of mastering the French language; and, by the admission of these others and their not so high opinion of us, the rebels, the reviled, the revisers and dimension hoppers – us, the collage artists and page polluters, they'd happily admit they assumed that we thought it was some alien language. It is though. As is the language we speak in foreign countries. We are all fecking aliens. Just some of us are Dadaists. Undermining that we Dadaists, collage creators are far more in the know, than they will ever know – you know? Nothing is original, not anymore, unless it is experimental and built upon such a great belief, with the devout coming out between the hours of ten o'clock at night and midnight, whilst not doing anything of the sort, at all – we create our own foundation – that, or merely create it amongst ourselves – alone, with a few buddies. We are original because we dare to face that criticism and vile accusation of plagiarism and appropriation - we are taking your work and destroying it – it could be Greek, broken Engrish. It is Latin. It is English. It is Japanese. Pekinese. It is Italian. It is universal – the printed image, the method of taking language, printed language and images and recreating reality. That is the foundation, and that is the heart, the core, the fucking brain of this ever0expanding artform. Collage is French anyway, of course we would know some French, wee-wee? *Collage (from the French: coller, "to glue" or "to stick together" is a technique of art creation, primarily used in the visual arts, but in music too,* (what about film?) *by which art results from an assemblage of different forms, thus creating a new whole. (Compare with pastiche, which is a "pasting" together.) A collage may sometimes include magazine and newspaper clippings, ribbons, paint, bits of coloured or handmade papers, portions of other artwork or texts, photographs and other found objects, glued to a piece of paper or canvas. The origins of collage can be traced back hundreds of years, but this technique made a dramatic reappearance in the early 20th century as an art form of novelty.* My words are collage elements. Ruined. Petulant. Oddly used and misused and totally fucking abused. My collage is my words and my method of understanding the world around me. Enough for me to say, the monotony of presence and perseverance is my mecca and safehold. Share these words. Resemble and reassemble and disappear in-between each line and cortisol-diabetic-pump! Share these words. This book will be in colour. It will be in standard. It will be available as colour and black and white, giving you an option. I might do this, I might not. Colour version. Colour aversions. Different names for the same book, hidden, I want to keep you on your toes. ISBN Mahna Mahna Do doo be-do-do Mahna Mahna Do doo be-do-do Mahna Mahna Do doo be-do-do Mahna Mahna Do doo be-do-do Mahna Mahna Do doo be-do-do monkeys that are pus lovers say, Mahna Mahna Do doo be-do-do Mahna Mahna say yes, and the Do doo be-do-do, Dada says no, but the Mahna Mahna says Do doo be-do-do – oh yes, David Tenant spitting. Frosted lens, oh, it is glaucoma. Cataracts as words. Words as anthrax. Mahna Mahna Do doo be-do-do Mahna Mahna Do doo be-do-do Mahna Mahna Do doo be-do-do Mahna Mahna Do doo be-do-do Mahna Mahna Do doo be-do-do Mahna Mahna Do doo be-do-do Mahna Mahna Do doo be-do-do Mahna Mahna Do doo be-do-do Mahna Mahna Do doo be-do-do Mahna Mahna Do doo be-do-do – end.

BROKEN MEN AND WOMEN SET THE RULES
THE RULES OF DERANGEMENT.

Lead poisoning. Teachers did nothing. *FUCK THEM. FUCK ALL OF THEM!* A deep sadness. Laugh. Acerbic. Caustic part and parcel of Autistic. Macro soul. Macro purpose. Microscopic qualities applied, to enforce an oval zoom, stretching it into a warped version of the tiny macro soul. In. Out. Around. Circles. Symmetry. Framed. Too big a heart. Little life experience to learn how to cope with these... sensations. Heart issues. Mind issues. Mentally ill. Perpetually depressed that I might as well move to Scotland and turn myself into The Black Dog. I need to laugh. I cannot laugh. I think my vantage point of this cruel place called home is brilliantly observed and still those I love most think I am weird and unfunny. Wastrel. Jobless. Dole-boy. Dole-boy. What you gunna do, what you gunna do when the benefits run out? Autistic, each year I, me, Zak must prove I am still indeed autistic. I am not normal. But in comparison to some others, I am peak normalcy wrapped up in abnormality. I am film. I am word. I am linguistics gone to shit. Housing crisis. No money. Less money. Things. Work. Job. Need to attain financial success. Why? Because, because, because... the wonderful jobless boy of Oz! Immune system is flawed. Scared 24/7 that I must be just a minor insect under the ever-threatening boot heel of an ant-bully. My carapace is my "autism" no it is my identity and humour. Laugh. Don't laugh. Cry. Always cry. I cannot cry. Tears are wasted on these attackers and molesters. Spots. Scabs. Picked. Poked. Healed. Healing. Re-infected. Delicious dinners. True love. My Laura. My everything. Undeserved. Smooth face strokes. Presence and essence keeping me safe and partially sane. But I do not provide this for her. I do. I don't. Love. Loathe. Me. Her. Politics is the new category to be seen as partaking in. Sweet child of mine. Ten in May. Miss him. Have no right to. I am weak. So weak. To be weak is to be human. Yes. Indeed, it is. Yet, it is still the bold-faced lies that she told to secure herself security, meaning free money and housing that annoys me. Father's have no rights. Unless they have green, green cash, blue, blue eyes, I will not meet my son again, until the day that I die, or cry. A child is not a pawn. No. It is not. It is my life essence. A distributed strand of myself. Bleeding heart. Rotten lungs. Coughing up the past lives' curses and ailments. Difficult. Abrupt. Abrasive. Leech. Worm. Slime. Bark. Textures. Sensations. Stimulation. Different modes of expression. Manic. Sparse. Breaking the epistemology known as the Zak effect. Systems break not to be reformed or reforged in the Amazon produced production of J.R.R. Tolkien's Appendices, but to be left to die out. Coffee. Sweeteners. Days gone. Months gone. Years flitting past as fast as the surrounding fields that frame and shape East Sussex. There. Observed. Never experienced in their full totality. Five more pages. Tummy rubs. Missing my childhood pals, the main man, Todd, and the main smelly ginger lady, Daisy. Pat. Spit. Cunt. Fucksake. Cuntforfucksake. Tic. Body taking over. Mind taking over. Body out of control. Replace by another tic, pushed in the corner for such situations. Tic. Pop ears. Bursting blood vessels in the eyes. Pop. Tic. Elastic body made rubbery made solid. Everything is starting to hurt. Aches up neck and around the shoulders. Books collected. No money sent. Give me money I keep sending free books what is wrong with me, do people not know I am brassic? Loops of infinity. Words. Page. Lines. Eyes. Follow. Redirect. Form. Create. Flourish. Zenith. Peak. Trials and errors. Errors and the corresponding trials. Low fluids. Sharp and strong squash, and a not so diluted orange squash making me cough up my lungs. Bottled. Pills. Popped. Piles dropped. No blood. Push. Orange is the new brown stain. Sleepy. Very sleepy. So tired of being tired. So exhausted of this exhaustion. Proud book Father. Neglectful book Dad. Book Mum is not part of the equation. Baby books passed from person to person. Not. Not really. Social services want to take my babies away from me, all because I haven't paid for them in over a month. Why should I? I created them. Silence. Just silence. Mere... drip, drip, drops, drops, of pear liquor. Pear drops. Murray mints. Mint humbugs. Chocolate. Cake. Fizzy piss and drinks. Feeling poorly. Feeling ill. Again, and again and again. Neglecting my body. Neglecting this passage. Gone. But never forgotten. Automatic writing is not the same as automatic drawing and auto-fiction is all fiction, it is all pouring from us. Unlimited film viewings, yet they are not unlimited as there are always rules coded into the system that you pay 17 squid/quid a month. No patience. Moody. Emotional. Tired. So very tired. The time is 12:04... I am about to get up to make a coffee before a house viewing... Bye... for now...

I am back, I have just finished a eating a sandwich I made - (with toasted bread) – filled with five slices of German salami, the toasted bread lathered in grainy mustard, the other slice lathered in light mayo, on ancient grain (toasted) bread, with my favourite filler-filler, sauerkraut – that I made knowing me and Laura are going to a viewing, and I had time, and I felt hungry, which is weird as my cravings for food really kicks in after 6:00pm or later/the coffee is instant, I'm not a coffee snob – I poured the kettle, doing various jobs related to making my brew and the sandwich – I can multitask, when it suits my needs/the various pickle flavours, and spices of the (toasted bread) sandwich, was sparking new life into me – which is strange, very strange, as food is food that gets mulched and "appreciated" – it is never ingested for the right reasons - but it is merely just eaten, not for taste but for the motion of mouth activity, the semblance it affords, the mental rewards, never forcing into focus that overeating at odd times is, well odd and unhealthy, that this is the perfect time to eat something in the day and not leave it until far too late in the evening - eaten, not because my body tells me it needs it, but because I tell myself I need it/no wonder I am getting fatter and fatter – I shove it in, that's my motto, this felt different, like a weird awakening, that my body actually needed the food, as I felt sluggish and hazy eyed and now I am alert, and damn it, I forgot to log when I returned to the writing seat – I believe it was 12:15 or later, 12:18, now it is 12:21. Not that you care. Who should. Minor observations are the bane of many a reader's existence. Guns pop. Lucid wet dreams that make you run home, hands groping your piss-tainted little willy-winkle. Crying all the way home to Mama. Dada isn't there. Mada is there. Mada as hell that you pissed your recently washed, and ironed, and heavily starched school trousers. *But Mada, but Mada!* you appeal – a slap sorts you out, and your hands uncover your wet patch, and the stain isn't green, like Mada thought it was, and ends up nestling you in her big buxom breasts, and you again add more wee to the damp patch, but due to the trousers colour, you are in luck, the spread doesn't change, that much, only this is sex-wee – added to your already sodden trousers. She does not want to listen to your snivelling. She retches down to feel the damp, you flinch, and then Mada realises you are now a big boy and get rock hard over any little thing, and the brush with her hand makes you come invisible fireworks and your Mother becomes Mada at you. Dada isn't here to save you. She strips you naked, and orders you to fight your erection. *But Mada, but Mada, I can't, you have big boobs, this is wrong I know, but Mada,* and to silence you, your excuses, and make you go limb she has swatted your erect cock (no bigger than 5cm) with her least favourite, clog-like slipper.

You never get a hard on again. That is all because Mada is wrong and Dada is always, always right.

(machine-gun-brrrrrbrattabratta-bratbrat-brrrrrbrattabratta-brat-brat brrrrr-bratta-bratta-brat-brats going off) - MICE ARE ON A BREAK!) squeeeek squeeeek, squeak squeak,

squeeeeeeeeeeak,

SQUARK!

Where did that duck come from?

MADA, I GOT AN ERECTION ... no not the slipper, anything

but that clog-like slipper, noooooooooooooooooooooooo

00000000

00000000

00000000

00000000

00000000

00000000

00000000

00000000

00000000

00000000

00000000

00000000

oooooooo

oooooooo

oooooooo

ooooo

Mada,

where is

Dada, oh fuck, nooooooo oooooooo oooooooo oooooooo

OOOOOOOO

OOOOOOOO

OOOOOOOO

OOOOOOOO

OOOOOOOO

OOOOOOOO

oooooooo

oooooooo

oooooooo

oooo - not

again.

INTERRUPTION.

NOTICE.

NONSENSICAL

VIGNETTES.

Autistic Break-Down waylaid.

"Fucking retard. Autism is a myth

and a lie," said [redacted]

INTER...

I cannot be bothered to even say, nor type it...

(Wait... then why did I write the – **INTER-** and not the rest of the **LEWD**?)

... (snooze button hit with such gusto it explodes into tiny amber coloured cogs and clockwork tinker-y bits and pieces) Guillermo Del Toro is proud, but still willing to sue... A

short-

abridged

collection

of

conversations:

"That is the point!"

"No. You guys are just not very imaginative."

"I think so".

"Fuck off Dad its none of your business!"

"I should have shot my load into her ass-cunt!"

... Tim Burton screwed up his plans and concept drawings, eying up his designs with autistic abandon - (meaning he couldn't even hold eye-contact of his products and creations, let alone human eye-contact)...

I wish Helena was here to sing a Sweeney Todd song! "Nothing is gunna 'arm you, not whilst I plague youuuuuuur films!"

... Tim looked at a part of a doodle not quite screwed up enough to hide his version of Apes.

Eyes missing the edges, far too close an engagement with something outside of his own reality... but the spirals, the scratched line-work enabled him to lean into his internal self, expostulated, made external by hand, pencil... scrap paper... imagination lives on page to be viewed; to view that of which should only be shuttered behind closed eyes and a Burton-y mind...

...The Apes looked emaciated and starved and very hairless and very lanky and very pale. But it was what Marky-Mark wanted, due to his now much wanted screen presence and appeal, and new-found resurgence... What Marky-Mark wanted for *Planet of The Apes: The Mark Wahlberg Dudier "HEY BRO!" Cut, was what he got!*

As life moves, crests, wavers, it saw change. Much to their chagrin. To their dismay. To their anger. To their utter discombobulation. They were powerless to evolution. It saw the cabins on Mars be replaced - no more Southern tastes lavished and appreciated. Prices altered, governments and councils from afar intervened. The semblance of what their sunny dust riddled town was, was soon to be lost to IKEA blandness. Even though their town, home, community on Mars was a carbon copy of any clichéd Old

Western Town, both structurally and aesthetically-

("Jon?"

"John with a H"

"John. Wayne. Good name."

"That it is.")

(minus a Gunslinger with a penchant for spitting)

It had in its own way altered, evolved. All except the sole centre and authoritarian family... The Martins. Stephen King wasn't disappointed, because his gunslinger was timeless, Idris Elba's wasn't/isn't. And the pay cheque helped numb the blow. At least he had a spot on the *It* special features, talking through it all offhandedly as if the millions weren't all fucking grinning about its fabulousness. A featurette dictated and fully dedicated to KING. Damn, what a great surname.)

(Ginger freckle faced director, a man who had strived to give the world the epitome of said Tower, that is a Dark magnum-opus of 7000-pages - a masterpiece, one that should have been translated in film- is flag waving again for attention to get it up and running.

Just for the space, that huge sparse dusty, though strategically contained dust zone-block on your living room shelf. That specific forlorn space. Remote Controlled syndrome attached to the future viewing.

Ronny Ron Howard: *"I wish I didn't spend my money on those Beatles songs for that documentary now, as I need that cash flow for MY ADAPTATION OF THE DARK TOWER, series!"*

Paul McCartney is laughing, because he filled Ronny Ron Ron's head up with the notion that the documentary was being made on a gentleman's handshake, and that all music used was included in the deal, for free, via said gentleman's handshake. Lying bastard, no wonder he turned cruel, eating all those fake sausages for so long.

Paul marched in with his cronies, thrust lawyers and music contracts upon Ronny Ron Ron Howard a few weeks before the film's release.

Never shake a Paul's hand. Not McCartney's and never Hollywood's, you have no idea where that hand has been, and whose snatch it has broken into.

Earning him – Paul McC $50 million in one hit, just so Ron didn't have a W A S T E D production.

... when, he had a long line up of various wasted productions already in his rear-view; many that go without any finality and no after-thought from anyone involved outside of Ronny Ron's wounded ego ... Oh all that money wasted... money having been put into the pre-production of this, that, the other... tallying up to not half the amount to bag them a legit CART-A-NAY-NAY OWNED song... to use... so the point of the story?

Ronny Ron-Ron, or merely Ronny Ron Ron Ron, got fucked over by Paul Mc-Cart-A Nay Nay-knob-end in favour of getting carte blanche to handle THE DARK TOWER FILM.

A potential new series by Stephen King looking close to some finalisation, oh yeah, if the film was a proven success.

It wasn't.

$60 million budget for a film that was awful... a burnt Ronny Ron-Ron Howard was left sitting in the only thing he had available that couldn't be taken off him (or so he thought, as this vintage vehicle was one, he took a liking to whilst filming American Graffiti with Lucas... but like with everything Lucas, does he needs to take what was originally his and pimp it out? And Lucas had been pondering upon what to do with that motor he had "loaned" Ronny-Ron after production wrapped). Ronny Ron Ron-Ron was left to cry.

Skint.

But, not all that much skint.

Just a tad skinter.

Poor guy, talented.

Wasted.

Then... from a Galaxy far, far away... (not that far from his own movie studios, which was at risk of being enveloped by the ever-expanding dominance of Dizzknee's buildings and various take-over constructions) ... Ronny Ron Ron-Ron was othered a chance of creative redemption.

A lot of money to make a wholly new film for Lucas Philmzzzzzzz...

"STA(e)R WARS? For me? Boooo-yeah-bitches! FUCK YOU PAUL MC-CART-NO-TALENT-NAY-NAY!" screamed Ronny Howard Ron Ron, up at the record company that Paul Mc Cart Nay No owned.

Somewhere in some Yellow-Submarine... (a Russian one no less), Paul Mc-Cart-Nay-Nay is living as he had every other day of his life, living it up as an absolute asshole, who was and is the most talentless of the Beatles, languishing in that knowledge but satisfied he was going to outlive them all. Left annually to continually be caught by whatever fellow-submariner wants to get a snap of him - wanking over a photograph of Yoko-Loco, Lennon's love child birthed a few months leading up to his death.

Paul still sniffs the guns barrel.

It was the closest he could get to being John Lennon.

OH!

COMING SOON TO A FUCKED-UP COMMUNITY NEAR YOU.

PART IV

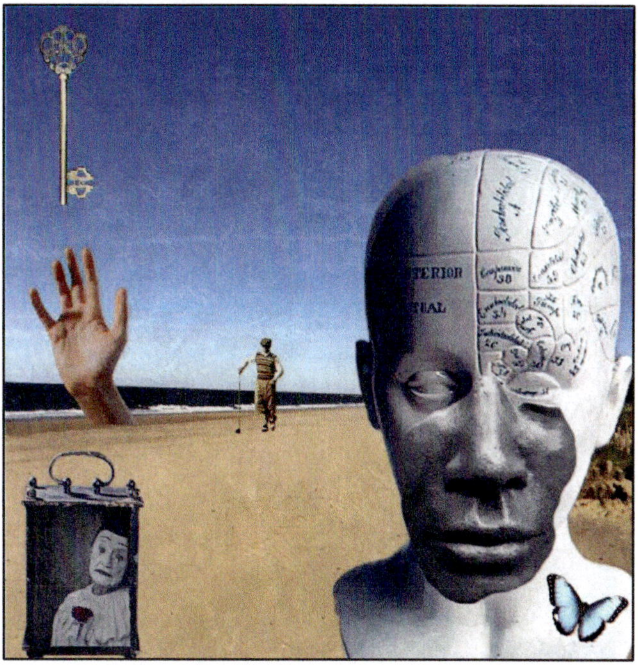

Let's traverse in a backwardly fashion...

Since those years, their pristine chapel had too been tampered by the times... *oh the times they are a-changing!* ... and it did indeed evolve into a glorious church ...

...Churches are empirical, beautiful, eerie, and totally pointless ...

...As evolution decides it, it grew into a revolution...

...Pistols had been drawn, fired, and blood had been sucked dry by the grit and sand, horses galloped and reared up mid gun fights, lives had been lost, the town had been plagued and robbed and visited by far off strangers...

...Swinging signs, dotted with forever smoking holes...

...Coffins leaning, with bodies nestled in, with as rigor mortised fingers than the survived Grand mommas in Town, often caught giving them the finger...

...Or between her grisled vulva lips, revealed to any wandering curious young-cow boy boot licking pleb...

...The ages went on...

...tarmac roads were grounded...

...homes built out of stronger things than wooden beams and the only consistency of the world and Town was its name and the Church erected...

...and those who followed by tradition and loyalty to their faith and family...

...they remained, heh, "loyal"...

...That was all that kept it historically and symbolically tied to its roots...

...By blood...

...By history...

...The strong hold of belief and prayer...

...Though often sneering at the alien nature that history had bestowed upon the generations of the town, the invent of television, music, high rising buildings that spread out like metallic wings to route off into other shallower depths of depravity, those lanes, high way roads, it still saw their home, their life, their Chapel of everything to do with "--------" - standing tall and proud as if kept safe in an invisible force field, untouched...

...Standing tall and prominent...

LOOMING. Forever present.

...Religion was feared, much feared, often mocked, but this Church held a benevolence of maligned evil...

...It focused on a much-maligned misinterpreted purity...

...The _____ purity...

...A purity that the world, naturally sort to end...

...Whatever came upon them in their years as a family and as the Religious Community - as it shifted and became a City, becoming a part of a broader map of the US of FUCKING amen! - it was not enough to detach their Christian Town's main forebears and faiths and leverages and strengths/stronghold over the land with its ever-expanding plots...

...In those dark days, in War, everyone in an afflicted state, with the fear and gluttony of need, for security, working its way through those not party to the real intentions of The _____, the weak had it plague their systems, working its way through them...

...Which itself worked in ways to help the _____. Gods' right-hand fam' – it played well into their oily hands...

It struck hard and that was when they knew their worth and their usages as a church and erected themselves, as the gracious all-knowing family that they told the masses that was what they needed...

Was it though? Was it NEEDED? Knowing they could curl their tendrils and swallow them up they took stock of the heightened mania. When grand issues of state and society happened, they knew that they would reach out and spread Gods word...

The word of God and Jesus through their filter. Spread through them, the Gospel of ______...

...That and (their interpreted) versions of Jesus's supposed scorn, and his fear!

...Reminding them as a species of their sinful ways...

...Able, working in tandem with each other, the cause, the effect, the fear, the belief necessary to numb such fear; like darkness to shadows and shadows to darkness, slow, groping, interspersing into one another to grow into a larger malevolence...

...To reach into their minds and extract that evil they had let rot and ingrain into their souls; both individually and hereditarily...

...An evil that is necessary for the human *id* to deal with and grow from...

The ills and weaknesses of a Community preyed upon by the ______...

...Accessed...

...Used...

...Abused...

...Manipulation the concurrent theme...

...Take the formal fears and spin them into something larger and more grotesque...

...Use what is happening to your advantage. People are always seeking hope or a realignment of self...

...Ignoring them as a Church and the years come to pass, within the walls of the Cult, the children of the _____ family line were not only drip fed their own form of alternate religious propaganda, but they were also given no time or breathing space to evolve into themselves and continue being their "religious" selves...

...Dedicated, devoted, loyal...

...Obsessed...

...The children knew nothing beyond their walls, and a given, if ever exposed to the growth of banality and impurity they would be dealt a stiff hand...

The children even outside of the _____ bloodline had been mentally brainwashed and driven to see all outside of their own take on Christianity

– the populace beyond their local, as sinners and nothing but filth.

...Filth they were as a community were compelled to cleanse...

...The _____'s used almost that nature of desperation and the need for some guiding light to their advantage...

...The despair, their existential crises exhumed from the people lending them a certain strand of purpose...

...Those looking for some tangible explanatory reason for their own aches, both as people and as long running familiars, tied to the local area by blood lines and some other variant of attachment to the Town, whether through history and association or not...

...Many hoping to shape the Town back into "their" hands and to become a mouldable form, for them to shape - back into its sacred almost hallowed reputation, alongside the holier than thou _____...

...To convert the unconverted that had invested their time, and money into building on their foundations and world, which was ______ ______ ______ ...

...To bring back the loss of those singulars, those who had lost faith, and those who had not taken to it like a baby to the tête, as they grew up into the forever expanding town, that was now no longer just dirt roads and a courtyard of cabins nor just the casual passing of varied structures, ovoid, rectangular, abstract, of the manic erection of the new age metal and brick work foundations, that dissolved and evolved as a Town does in the years in flux...

...The occupants of [redacted] were generally laid back and unconcerned to the age of change, but it bothered the, taking away what was theirs, from the beginning...

...With change of structure was change of populace and people, ushering in differed lifestyles and choices when in a Town like [redacted] there should have only been one of Christian "[redacted]-Skewed" faith...

...The townsfolks and their eagerness converging into ignorance of the change that comes in the wake of every Revolution was allowing structures to be erected and along with it was an erection of trouble and sin...

...That was laid down in stone and concrete and metal...

...A web-work of avenues and hidey-holes that the [redacted] family couldn't infiltrate and scout out and lay claim to, by virtue and history alone...

...Whilst also now becoming part as the onesome/expendable America, by craft and map expansions...

...The [redacted] Christian faith losing its original soulful aura that comes with its Town and environ, lost to the new age that by structure also came along with new religions, new eager admonishments, new creeds, new races, even ever more juicy sinful acts/persuasions that would see it BEING broken and destroyed...

...Though not their religion and belief...

They had to have that, The [redacted] or they would have either fallen into purgatory- the place that was growing around them with every day they grew more twisted and eaten up by their arrogance and delusion.

...They would have fallen foul to Gods own administrative slap for their own fraying ideals and absolutions to keeping his message and influence well-greased and forever processed and indoctrinated into minds, now willing to expand beyond that of which the [redacted] couldn't nor would ever willingly escape from...

... So, when challenging times struck way back, The [redacted] though in their best manner, deluded, confounded, greedy for prayers-ways (that was almost beneficial to them to fuel their own continuation of dedication) that when those times came, they allowed those peasants of sinful thoughts, acts, sodomite behaviours and undoubted alienation, to come and beg for forgiveness...

...And come they did, clamouring when WAR raged, or some form of dislocation had befallen the local area or nation, its influence and politics somehow being integrated without the [redacted] family's say-so...

...As a family and as the peak of the region's religious hierarchy, they picked up those (which had been most of, and much of the town when either bridled with death, decease and famine) they had explored religion with their newfound/newly lost children...

... To "show" them the right way, the only way to redemption and good living; of good will and righteous deeds that enhanced and induced them...

...Converted them...

...Brought them back onside...

...Guilt tripped...

...Mental abuse...

...Fearmongering...

...Vicious punishments and admonishments...

THEY WOULD BE THERE, AND ONLY BE THE ONES TO TURN TO.

The [redacted] would give them *a sense of* worthiness and sanity, by *belief*, installing that, "yes they be Gawwwwds children" and "there should be a fear, for what was to be taken from us all *in* our time on this hallowed plain of existence!" *Their* livelihood was all about (faux) love of the children, of human *sanity*; the people who could only be the one's able for such offerings of place and *worth* for they had been lost, their flock of lambs *going* wayward to return emaciated and in need to be fed up (with bullshit) and dealt an *easy* hand of ignorance, but, would be forgiven, *if only they* rise as one voice and oppose that of which had *struck* their iron hearts, to smelt into putty for the lord to pick *up* and pull a blacksmith feat of absolute *immortal solidification*. Everything to become anew along with their *shattered* souls. Rooted to the belief they feared for their fellow *townsmen*/woman/bastardy demon children, what it also *came down to*, was their need for these people, "their" people; for "their" approval again, for notification and notoriety, for them to admit to *the heavens* that by the years passed, that their dedication to the Lord and "everyone's" saviour, that the [redacted] had given an elevated truth. *That they were* needed and relevant, as relevant as the Lord and his almighty words themselves. *Giving* back what the Town and God himself had lost. That they as a religious family and his servants were right in their stance *to* continue to hold onto the ground that shook and quaked, from tufty grass to grit and sand *to* paving stones and to gleaming tarmac, that they had remained there for the people, readied with their God and willing to *help* guide his unwise misguided children. To be bathed in that golden holy ray of lord lord lordly light, that only *the religious* or those that spread his Gospels and atonements knew of. That ushered emotion, that feeling, glorified! - by their guidance, a pathway to the most-right wing *way* of life, giving them also food for thought (brainwashing still a stipulation to their execution) implanting a deeply seeded fear into them, *in hope it would* coil and solidify. Guiding them into their readied open arms, with a few psalms and soliloquys weighted by their utter zealotry and affirmed place alongside God - whispered into their ears, trickled like *warm* treacle into their brain-piece. To remain *Gods* voice for their common man/woman and child... **DO YOU REALLY CARE FOR THIS NARRATIVE STRAND?** that by standing an order/Church along with their flair of radiant all- knowing light (that was and could once again be erected as tall and solitary as they were, but still positive in their stance that God would see to it by "their" good deeds done and constant hand clasping was appreciated and conformed to, with their eyes a peeled to the skies followed by whispered breathes and prayers, nipples erect, areolas as thick and firm in erection, cocks hardening over the virgin Mary's whore like methods though still retaining – purity - crosses inserted, gyrated upon, cum trickling, like off milk Momma... downwards, coating the cross in a new paint job, that they would as the local saviours, the prophets of their agenda... Then again, time moved on and they as a family and as a righteous notable Christian Church were now nothing more than something that was on the maps to gloat at and to wax lyrical about. About its age-old patronage and history. What it once stood for, and why it truly was kept erect and solid up on its old wood rotten structures.

Indeed, it stood for something. **DID IT? DOES IT?** A death of ages yet forever at heel, to when the men and woman have plague riddled flesh and need an excuse to nuke the rats hive over yonder. And:

IT IS A LAZY WRITER WORKING AS A LAZY-WRITING-MACHINE WORKING TO WORK FOR THE SAKE OF WORK – WORKING IN NOTHING – NUFFINK! TO SUBVERT ADD FULFIL A NEED

TO JUSTIFY EMPTY DOCUMENTS LEFT ALONE – to die a death - DUSK BLOOD SOAKED IN THE DIGI-TAE-LITUS. RATHER

TRUTHFUL TO MULTIPLY THE TRUTH OF THE MATTER OF BEING LEFT, OR USING WASTE NOT WANT NOT, THAT SIDE OF THE EQUATION,

OF COURSE NOT, DO NOT TROUBLE YOURSELF.

NOTHING MAKES SENSE.

EVERYTHING DOES, that it was something to look back on and muse upon, as to what it meant in those days and how contrasting it was to the evolving of the times itself. The town of ----- was now a city, living its own strange ulterior life - its only living form consisting of walking personifications of: commercialism, sex, lust, perversions, neon lights, districts, strips to guide you to sin, take out porn like take away... except greasier in hand... weight giving over to sweaty armpit seediness, dripping ugliness, paper and digital contracts that branched into contracts of flesh, of holes being prodded and abused and sored, varied perspectives - it was not the [redacted] way, much to their tempered chagrins. . . boarded by valleys and mountains like before, this time only spotted with lights, tarmac gleaming roads, hotels and now the building, the place, the core of their delusions and obsession, was not so lonely, no longer possessing a peak, that had corroded down with time as did the rest of the locales - who were now nothing but dust - this now being a city, hustle that bustle, a bustle with sinners, blacks, gays, perverted murderers and paedophiles like all great notorious places. A place where fifty other places were accessible by free-way or sub-way and posed as a Church.

Blah! The only remaining person of lineage of blood and time, a moving of what once was a small solitary town, was [redacted] himself, lost in his own fashioned beliefs.

BLAH BLAH

BLAH BLAH

BLAH BLAH

BLAH BLAH

BLAH BLAH

BLAH BLAH

BLAH BLAH

BLAH BLAH

BLAH BLAH

BLAH BLAH

BLAH BLAH

BLAH BLAH

BLAH BLAH

BLAH BLAH BLAH BLAH

Crosses thrust at his face as if a tester to his night flesh, not yet in decomposition.

BLAH BLAH BLAH BLAH

A crashing of pebble to flesh. Crackling tin foil foibles. Cooking up a nice greasy spoon. Fat of the flesh. Fat of the addiction. Fat wads of cash. Dirty, well palmed. Well-lived. Well passed on. Well spent. Well accumulated. Willy Wanked over. Sticky. Green. Smog. The desolation of cash. The burning of trees. The burning of a lush rain forest and such. Oil. Industrial diggers. Puffing gases. Imprinted upon the cash-load.

Palms – the size of atoms – the size of stars - the huge truckers smashing and uprooting and staining the once beautiful fresh pure environment into a polluted soot-riddled scorched hollow. A damn bombsite. A crater. Created by palm. By greed. For that green that fills pocket and not soul through your eyepiece with the settling chirrups of nature resolving that, “oh man, it could not get any better”. Nature. Nurture. Burn it all for more soot ladled money. Soot-ladled into the homeless m(a)en’s proffered bowls - to be filled of what they are deserving of. Rich stay rich. Poor get poorer or get dead. Poor get fatter. Rich get fitter. Peasants’ fat and glutenous, affordable food just junk food. Healthy food and natural derivatives only bestowed upon the $$$ ching!ching!ching! masses. Screaming gesticulating children, with melting sticky sticks, of stuff that could only be best waxed upon by its visage as crystallized human matter, twisted and enforced, popped, curdled, variants of chemical wizardry given over to satiate such sweet cannibalistic sweet cragged broken oozing gum appetites. Succulent. Baby. Legs. Chopped up. Tender pudgy flesh. Made sweet by the addition of self-evolved and called for by delusion and self-righteous ego patheticism to make that cheap herb and spice, isn’t it all rather nice, to taste, rather, nice-nice. Because there’s nothing like buying herbs and spices to spruce up your meal-time delicacies and dishes and it turns out to taste like fucking shit. That or it worsens something intended to be improved upon. Improve. Cannibalistic tendencies. Cut off that sentence. Paper sailor caps, fish and chips stains imprinted upon their flesh, greasy paper-print, fish oils transferred from paper to fish and chip carrier/plate to the food, to then the not so much imprint - having been imprinted, *but, oh yes,* there is always a-but, *BUT*! - but allow it to bloom on their faces, like stylized tattoos; bending into malformed frames to then be exposed to tall erudite Nazi's with trench coat lapping at the stem of their tall gangly legs. Radar. Dish. Nipple licked. It's pointing towards a spark of flint to cock and cock to flint, cock to gravel, igniting a charcoal texture of flakes, shedding revealed was a roughhewn shaft. Foreskin reduced to thick rubbery slathers of flesh, tearing in deep trench marks, lean in and see the cowering British with uniforms dirty with fear, sweat, blood, viscera, stains of their pre-ejaculation due to the tremors rising up from the foundations they find themselves - cowardly - hiding – fatigued - and smoking nasty smokes made of whatever could be reduced into particulates that is akin to tobacco by design; coating themselves in comrade broken flesh, with sheds of their newly reissued flesh, as hiding veils, knowing a huge Godlike, leathered, emblemed swastika clad gloved hand is waving in their direction, foretelling their extinction - igniting the children not so much to morph in strange alterations of aesthetic, but it just happens, akin to a rapid cut of time and in an artistic manner, that would be much credited in cinema, but not so much in fiction or in reality, all due to discombobulation and acceptability to the unevolved human mind; that in its growth, whether demented or autistic or ignorant, a subconscious control still aligns what's right and what isn't within their conception of time and do's and don'tssssss and progressionsssssssah! **SIRE!**

DEAR!

WORMWOOD!

Decompartmentalization happens. It is natural influence. Natural need to understand the world. That jump and cut is why drugs are turned to. To leak the departments, to alter their current states. But if a natural cut of time and transition akin to that has been groomed and kept, as only available through cinema or if a drug user/as a drug user, it is quite uncomfortable... All these cock sparks. Fire popping off. Taking him off his feet and transporting him to the other side of town in its furious explosion of thrust and pedal to the fucking metal. New-Metal Scum. Punk Rock vibes getting our shit-kicks, so as our bums can excrete that crum to be dustpan and brushed up into a maw wanting to eat and break down the excrement into particulates known only between shifting, and only found within, cellular animation.

Larry & Barry: Builders and Contractors. The best of chums. Grew up on the same council estate. Both fended for themselves, and only ever had each-others back, when not truly pinned or outnumbered. They fought their own battles. If it affected them as a duo, it would be dealt with, just as is. Either solely they dealt with it on their own terms and conditions and their own ways. Both were brothers, partners. They earnt a living. They were never selfish, they thought as a duo. If one had an idea another would always encourage and do whatever it took to get it off its feet and ensured that it could be furthered. They were the cliched builder bloke broh's on the street. Both in their fifties, with no retirement in sight. No wives. No children. Just work. Social lives outside of work hours and odd weekends, but they were so consumed by their work often paperwork was a weekend designation for both the 'Arry's. They worked as a duo. No one has nor would ever edge into their own "enterprise". Though, in this fable there was a time when Larry decided to cut Barry out. Not out of disinterest, maliciousness or ulterior motives that could be assumed as a negative influence on their future as partners and friendship; but because Larry was diagnosed with testicular cancer. He had treatments. This was the time where we saw Larry isolate himself. Disappearing to private appointments, having not wanted Barry involved with seeing him go through the ringer and ultimately, see him slowly deteriorate. So, he decided upon to keep it from him. But, by doing so, keeping these new trial runs, and going too far out, secreted locations and destinations, to himself, it did create a short-lived dip in communication and contact. But Larry found a way to explain THIS AWAY. So heartily comfortable that THEY WERE, it took not much time for this gap to be filled. Comfortable amongst each other - a hug, even as bear-like and rough, masculine, and affirming in their friendship/and companionship, there is always a tenderness. Either one, or most cases simultaneously reach out a hand, resting it on either or on each other's shoulder. A slight squeeze of reassurance.

"I can't go out to a night-club".

“Why not?”

“I just can’t... look, it’s a bit of a touchy subject for me, awright- Barry?! Yeah?! Yeah, well shut yer mush!”

“Fine. Fine.”

“Oh alright. The thing is mate... I, uh, **HARRUM** strobe lighting gives me an erection.”

“Pffffttttttt!”

“Tea hot, Barry?”

“No, I was, oh, never mind.”

“I just get real rock-stock-hard. Not a pointer enough to impress the night-club masses, as most of them out there are, *well*, you know! They’re all high on life and the smell of fresh pussy is their amassed aim, and use it, the um, proverbial hardy, as a, you know, um, as a Sexual-Douser-Rod to the freshest pussy available, or um one that’s still available in sight that aren’t drenched in post-quim-gush. But mine is a tad, uncomfortable. He, also, recently gets a bit vocal.”

“Whuh?!”

“Barry. Strobe lights get me hard. Then my cock gets, boulder-ised almost, he goes rubbery, then hard then... look in builders’ terms it all starts as a cement mix... then it hardens on its own terms."

"Right?"

"And it sings..."

"What does it sing? Is it like a jukebox?"

"Fuck off!"

"Okay, but seriously... what does it sing?"

"Sweet Caroline."

That was the day they both parted ways.

To this day the cock sings that song and the cock owner 'Arry of the once 'Arry duo cries himself to sleep.

At least he no longer had cancer.

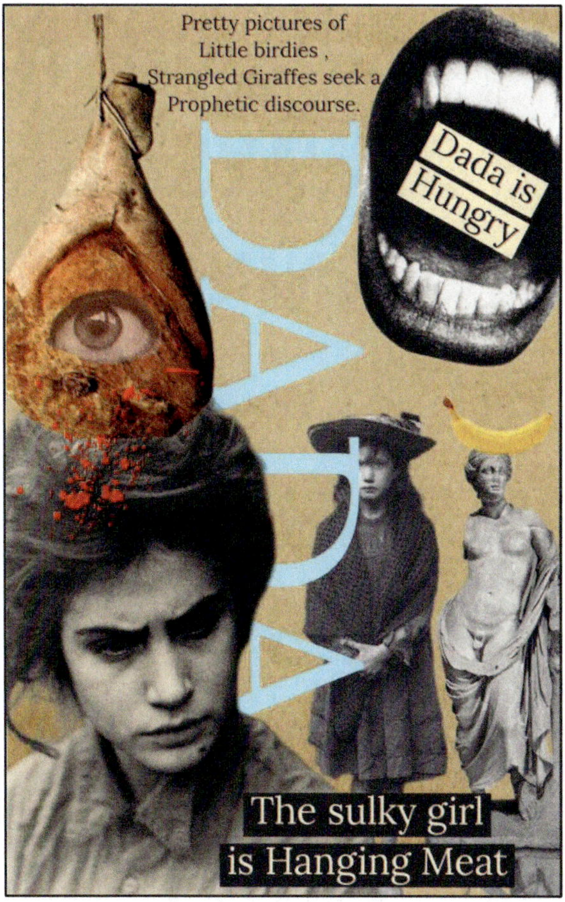
Pretty pictures of
Little birdies ,
Strangled Giraffes seek a
Prophetic discourse.
DADA
Dada is
Hungry
The sulky girl
is Hanging Meat

THIS MIGHT BE THE END, BUT IT IS ALWAYS THE BEGINNING. THE BEGINNING USHERS IN A STRONG SENSE OF – IS THAT IT?

IS THAT ALL? NO, IT IS NOT OVER. NO.

THIS IS A MANIFESTO WITH NO LIMIT AND NO PURPOSE OTHER THAN,

THE SEDIMENTS OF PAST LIVES HAS CORRODED YOUR inner ego enough FOR YOU NOT TO REALISE THAT THE CAPS LOCK

TURNING ITSELF ON/OFF IS GETTING A LITTLE BIT FUCKING ANNOYING. END THIS PAGE BEFORE IT IS

TOO LATE FOR US!

THE END

FOR

NOW

ABOUT THE AUTHOR:

NOTHING.

HE IS A TWAT!

ABOUT THE ARTIST:

MYSTERIOUS.

LEGENDARY.

IMPRESSIVE.

LUCID.

A DADA DREAM.

SDP
SWEAT DRENCHED PRESS